SURVIVALIST

BOOT

CAMP

Ruthie Lenor

ruthielenor.com

Published by Honeybells Publishing
Edited by A.K Edits
Cover Art by Ruthie Lenor

ISBN: 9780578842165

First Edition

SURVIVALIST

BOOT

CAMP

CHAPTER 1

"**I** would love to send you some more, dear."

"You are too sweet, Mrs. Coleman, but we really couldn't accept another case of chocolates." Faye Morris looked to the bookshelf on her right, silently sighing. Instead of seeing neatly stacked spines of books, it was filled with cases of Coleman chocolates in all different varieties. As Mrs. Coleman's voice blared through the speakerphone on her desk, Faye had to fight the urge to laugh as her writing partner sat across from her at his desk, popping Coleman peanut clusters in his mouth. He'd just tilted his head back and caught one when she pressed the mute button midway through Mrs. Coleman's droning. "I hope you choke, you know that?"

"...but I just wanted to call to thank you for such a great article. If it hadn't been for you and Izzy, I don't know if I would still be in business."

Faye grinned, then said, "You're very welcome, Mrs. Coleman. We were just doing our jobs."

The story Mrs. Coleman was talking about featured the 50-year history of the small local business which had sold chocolate for almost three generations. To get a better feel of the process, Faye and her partner learned to make dozens of different batches of candy, sampling everything they made. By the time the story was printed, Faye didn't want to hear the word cocoa. The article was so well-read, business picked up more than Mrs. Coleman expected. She had to hire more employees to keep up with demand, and in the end, profits skyrocketed. To show her thanks, she started sending cases of chocolates to the office, c/o Faye Morris. The first box she took home, she ate all thirty-six pieces in one night. She blamed it on PMS-ing while watching Love Jones. The bloated feeling she felt the next day had her so miserable, she hadn't touched the chocolates since.

"Okay, dear. I'll let you get back to work. I'll talk to you soon."

Faye picked up the receiver on her phone then dropped it back down to hang up. She rested her head on her desk, then groaned. "Next time, you talk to her."

"She likes you better."

"How do you know?" Faye asked, her head still on her desk.

"She's never said your name wrong." Faye lifted her head, looking at her partner, Dizzy, who Mrs. Coleman had renamed Izzy. "Face it, Faye, all the old ladies like you."

Picking up a stack of papers, Faye tapped them on her desk to straighten them out, then placed them in a tray. "Jealousy isn't a good look for you, Dizzy."

Dizzy Freeman had shared an office with Faye for five years, sitting across from her since day one. He shrugged, knowing she was kidding. "You want some chocolate?" he snidely offered, already knowing the answer.

Working side by side with him for years, Faye knew he wasn't jealous. He liked to tease her sometimes. The chocolates were a low blow. "Are you done with those edits yet?"

"Almost," he answered, then used his tongue to wipe bits of chocolate and peanut off his gums. He took a large gulp of water, then hit a few keys on his keyboard. "All done." He smiled, showing off the dimple high on his right cheek.

Faye adjusted her yellow beaded necklace, making sure it lay perfectly against her green floral top. "Why do I even put up with you? We could have turned this in two hours ago."

Dizzy gave her a small smile before taking another sip of water. "You've been on the phone for thirty minutes, so I couldn't send it to you. This is your fault."

Faye pointed to her monitor, indicating he send it to her so she could add it to the layout. "What time is the meeting today?"

"Don't know. I haven't seen Shannon lately." Dizzy stood from his chair to stretch his back, leaning his 6'4" height to the left, then the right. "Come to think of it, I haven't seen much of anyone today."

They worked on the eighteenth floor of a high-rise building in downtown Fort Worth. The magazine they wrote for occupied two floors, with writers, editors, photographers, and anyone else who was involved with a magazine. Working from home wasn't unheard of, so when the office seemed empty, Faye assumed people were doing their job from the comforts of their home. Faye rarely worked from home because the one time she did, she discovered that when her family found out she was at home, they took it to mean she had time to talk or do things that didn't pertain to her job.

"Oh, well, she'll probably show up in a minute since I mentioned her name." Her eyes scanned the screen of the monitor, checking that everything flowed the way she wanted it to. Even though they had editors, she and Dizzy had their own section of the magazine they were responsible for. Her controlling nature made it hard to relinquish creative control to others, so when the option to do it all was placed on the table, she grabbed it up as fast as she could. "This is missing something," she said, looking over at Dizzy.

He knew that look meant he needed to get up to give his input. "Well," he said, leaning down to get a closer look at her screen. "Move this picture of the trees—it's too green. Then change the color of this font." He underlined the word with his finger then stood back up smugly.

"Now, I have to clean my screen." She looked up at his face, his afro making him seem taller than he already was.

"You were about to clean it anyway," he said, going to sit back down. She was, but she didn't need Dizzy rubbing in her obsessive need for a sparkling computer monitor. The phone rang, and they both looked at the number on the small screen. "It's for you," he laughed.

With a groan, Faye answered the phone, using the speaker again. "Faye Morris."

"Faye, honey, why do you insist on having me call you on your office phone? I'm your mother, for God's sake."

Faye looked to the ceiling for strength. It was always the same thing with her mom. "I'm at work, mom. I have work hours."

Francine Morris was a licensed clinical psychologist. She was literal and loving with her opinions when she wanted to be, never biting her tongue or sugarcoating how she felt about anything, even her disappointment in her oldest daughter Faye. Their most mundane conversations always turned into a session, with Francine analyzing all of Faye's decisions. Faye was surprised she didn't find bills in her mailbox. "I really hope you fix that soon."

Fixing that meant working from home full-time, or better yet, marrying rich, so she didn't have to work at all. Faye had no interest in fixing anything. "Did you need something, Mom?"

"Of course, I do." Faye could hear the transition in background sounds. Francine was walking from outside to inside. "I'm at that cute little boutique on Weston Avenue and wanted to know if you wanted me to pick you up anything."

"That's very nice of you, mom, but I don't need anything." Faye tapped her nails on her desk, hoping the conversation would be over soon.

"Are you sure? What are you wearing Friday night?"

Faye stopped tapping as she dropped her nails to the smooth surface, then quickly pulled up the calendar on her computer, searching for what Friday night was. She prided herself on remembering things, so she wasn't sure why Friday night had slipped her mind. The small square on her calendar was blank—not even a holiday or full moon reminder was in it. "What's Friday night, mom? I don't have anything on my calendar for that night." She could see Dizzy's eyes looking at her, trying to figure out what she'd forgotten.

Francine blew out an exasperated breath, making sure Faye heard the entire huff. "It's the quarterly mixer at the club, honey. I swear, Faye, what would you do without me?"

Faye chewed down on her tongue before answering. "I'm not going to the mixer."

"What? Why?"

"Because I hate those things. I don't feel like rubbing elbows with your club pals or fake-laughing at jokes while sipping champagne," Faye sighed. "I told you after the last one I wasn't going to another mixer."

"I figured you'd have changed your mind since then, Faye, honey. I don't understand why you don't want to go."

"I just told you." Faye closed her calendar, bringing her attention back to the work on her monitor. "I have to get back to work, mom. I'll call you later, okay?" Without waiting for a reply, Faye hung up, assuming her mother knew 'later' meant 'sometime next week.'

"So, your mom's doing good?" Dizzy asked. Faye glared at him. "You want me to call her back and tell her, not only are you not going to some mixer, whatever that is, you're also looking at me all mean? Your nostrils are flaring." Dizzy raised an eyebrow as she continued to glare at him. "You're like a dragon with an afro." Faye balled two sheets of paper together then pitched as hard as she could, aiming for his head. He caught it one-handed then tossed it in the trash by the door. "Nothing but net, baby!"

The phone rang again, and Faye answered it before looking. It was her sister Freya. Faye hung her head, knowing it couldn't be anything good since she'd just hung up with their mother. "Hey, what's up, Freya?"

"You know what's up. Your mother called fussing about you not going on Friday. Why didn't you tell her?"

"My mother?" Whenever there was an issue, Francine was always given to Faye. "I told her the night of the last one I wasn't going again." After a long night wearing shoes too cute to waste on the quarterly mixer, Faye told Francine that was her last time going to anything at the club involving more than ten people.

"Well, she either didn't believe you or thought you changed your mind. Faye, you know you have to hammer these things into her. You should've been telling her." Faye heard a thud, which meant Freya was either pounding on the table she was sitting at or the wall she was leaning on. "Every day for the past three months," Freya whined out. "Why are you doing this to me?"

"I'm not doing anything. I told her. Now, if she conveniently forgot, that's on her, not me." Faye looked over at Dizzy, mimed grabbing a knife, then stabbed it through her chest. "You know why she wants me there, right?"

"Can't you just indulge her?"

"No." The one-word answer was all Faye was going to say. She was tired of explaining to everyone, including her little sister, why she didn't want Francine Morris playing matchmaker for her, trying desperately to introduce and hook her up with every club member's son, nephew, or frat brother's wife's best friend's cousin. She could hear Francine in her ear. *"You're forty years old, Faye, don't you think it's time to settle down?"* Her mother didn't understand—forty was too old to settle for anything.

"Fine," Freya responded. She knew she wasn't getting more.

"Where's Jason? You know he's my favorite out of all y'all." Saying Jason's name immediately lifted her mood. Her three-year-old nephew was about the only one she liked all the time. He was easy. Juice, a good movie, and cuddles made him happy. Faye could handle that.

"He's asleep. I'll tell him you asked about him." They both went quiet, leaving only the sounds of Freya's breathing. "You sure you can't go?" Freya questioned one more time.

"I'm not going, Freya!"

"Fine. I'll talk to you later."

"Gotta get back to work, anyway. Love you."

"Love you too, Sis."

CHAPTER 2

"Look, all I'm saying is, it doesn't make sense for you to have three when you don't even use one."

"Do you want one?"

"I mean, if you're offering, Diz, I'll take one."

"I bet your begging ass will." Dizzy sat on his couch in front of his TV, headset on, focused on scoring a touchdown against his opponent Sean. Their morning Xbox game happened every Tuesday and Friday between the friends who'd met freshman year of college. Eighteen years later, they still talked almost every day. "When are you gonna stop believing you can beat me at this game? It's starting to get embarrassing." Dizzy's thumbs and pointer fingers worked to move his player through Sean's defense for a hard-fought 6 points. The score was 42-12, with one quarter left to go. "There's nothing wrong with cutting your losses."

"Is that the line you used on Stacy? Or was it Tracy?

Dizzy knew what Sean was up to and had expected this turn in the conversation. His older-by-seven-months friend, who was also wiser, always used their games as the time for a heart-to-heart. Last time, it was his career goals. Today, his love life drew the short straw. "Not all of us can meet the girl of our dreams the first day of freshman English then marry her the week after graduation. Some dreams take a little longer to manifest."

"You don't think thirty-seven is old enough to settle down?"

Intercepting Sean's pass with a laugh, Dizzy answered, "Why is it 'settle down', though? Why can't I meet the woman I'm meant for and live a happy, chaotic life, flying through the air or something?"

Sean laughed into his headset. "Your life isn't chaotic, though. You wake up promptly at 6:30 every morning, lift weights after you play Xbox, take a long shower, then go to your job."

"Right now, my job is kicking your ass in this game," Dizzy answered, setting down his controller. The game was over. Another win in his column. He heard Sean sigh. "Look, if it makes you feel better, I'm taking a break from dating for a while. I can't stand the setups or the awkward first dates anymore. I'm gonna chill for a bit."

He was tired of the audition process. Pick a girl up, go out on a date, make sure doors are opened, and the hand at the small of her back doesn't graze too low or too long. Stand close enough to seem interested, but not close enough to seem creepy. Laugh at jokes that make no sense and smile when she looks at you even if you don't want to. By the end of the night, he was way too exhausted to do anything but walk her to her door and kiss her on the cheek. Pretending wasn't what he wanted to do to fall in love. He wanted an easy, organic love. In his dream of dreams, he would look up, and there she'd be. The One.

"Or you could finally tell fine-ass Faye what the deal is," Sean said.

Dizzy reached down under his coffee table to pick up one of

his weights to start bicep curls. "Nah, it's not the right time. I want to worry about only me for a while."

"Chicken," Sean teased. "Have you at least told her about your plan?"

"No," Dizzy answered, continuing with his reps until he got to thirty, then switching arms. Before he could explain, his phone glowed with a call. "Say, man, my sister's calling. I gotta go."

"Bet."

"Hey, Ella," Dizzy answered, keeping his breathing steady. "What's up?"

"Workout time, huh? You know they have gyms for that? Keeps your house from smelling like sweat and funk." Her laughter didn't amuse him at all. He stood up and brought the weight above his head to start on his triceps.

"If you don't have anything productive to say, then put Billie on." Ella's sigh came through the phone, making Dizzy laugh. His big sister knew not to annoy him, or he'd default to uncle instead of brother mode. His niece Billie was six and possibly the smartest, brightest person he knew. "Is she there?"

"Dizzy, can you answer my question before you start ignoring me?" He set down his weights, wiped the sweat from his forehead, and waited for Ella to continue. "Okay, well, I want to order some g-i-f-t-s," Ella whispered so Billie wouldn't hear. "But I need to send them to your place. I don't trust these people around here." Ella lived in an upscale neighborhood with a neighborhood watch plus Nextdoor, which meant someone was always watching. They looked out for each other, but they also looked out for UPS, FedEx, and USPS. Dizzy knew there had to be a secret sect of the neighborhood watch who only tracked the number of packages people got delivered to their porches.

"How many boxes?"

"Only six, but they're not big. Can I?"

He sat quietly for a few moments, icing her out, frustrating her on purpose. There wasn't much he wouldn't do for his sister, but annoying her before he agreed to anything was par for the course. She should be used to it. "Sure, Sis. Where's Billie?"

"Ugh! You get on my nerves."

Satisfied, Dizzy switched his phone to video so he could see Billie. "Hi, Uncle Diz!" She'd lost one of her front teeth, so the Z in his name was cutely hissed out.

"Good morning, Billie Bug. What's going on today?" Her smile always grew when he called her Billie Bug. The deep dimple right below the left side of her bottom lip he swore she got from him magnified whenever he did.

"Oh, nothing. I had to clean my room, and we made my shirt for the carnival. Are you going?"

"I'll be there." The fall carnival was all Billie talked about lately. She'd been put in charge of the dunking booth and was currently recruiting dunkees for the day. Dizzy had enthusiastically declined, blaming his hair's aversion to unknown water. "I'm about to feed Cecily and Miles. You want to help me?"

"Yes!" Dizzy turned the camera to face his fish tank and the two bettas who swam the length of it all day. Eight months ago, he got the sudden urge to get a pet. He looked up the best pets for people in apartments, the best pets for singles, even the best pets for people who aren't pet people. He had almost put the idea out of his mind when he discovered the bettas in a shop window walking to lunch one day. Cecily was an elegant lavender color with fluffy fins that started at the top of her head all the way around until they reached the bottom of her head.

Miles was blue. A deep navy covered his body and fins with
cerulean streaks along his tail. "Miles, have you been behaving?"
Billie asked. The perpetually unemotional fish swam to the glass
to look at the face that was talking to him.

"I don't know how you do it, Billie, but I think he's smiling."
Dizzy sprinkled the dried bloodworms into the tank, then
watched Miles swim away to get his breakfast. "He's never
smiled at me."

"Fish can't smile, Uncle Dizzy," she laughed while watching
the fish swim around.

Dizzy changed the view of the camera, so his face was now
on the screen. "They do it all the time. It looks like this." He
sucked in his cheeks to create a fish mouth with his lips, then
tried his best to make a smile. He knew it wouldn't work, but he
wanted to hear her laugh again. It worked.

"You're silly," Billie said between her laughs. "Fish don't look
like that."

"Oh, yes, they do." He made the face again, this time
moving his head from side to side to make it look like he was
swimming.

"I hope your face sticks like that," Ella said, taking the
phone from Billie. Dizzy shrugged but didn't drop his fish face.
"We have to go. Got more shirts to make. Say bye to your uncle,
Billie."

"Bye, Uncle Dizzy!" They both waved at the camera, then
ended the call.

Shedding his clothes on his way to take a shower, he was
naked by the time he turned on the faucet. While he waited for
the water to heat up, he checked his face in the mirror,
inspecting his skin, ensuring the face scrub he'd started using
was doing its job. At his age, he was starting to notice the signs
of aging caused by hours outdoors. He didn't mind the gray

that sprouted from his head and face. He liked the way his afro looked with the sprinkling, his beard too. With steam starting to escape from behind the shower curtain, he got in and started his routine.

Dizzy loved his morning showers, which was why he waited until after his Xbox game to take one. Showers were not to be rushed. Despite his laid-back attitude, as his mother called it, he actually paid very close attention to his appearance. He might be wearing a thrift store shirt, but his socks nestled inside his cowboy boots were always designer, bought from the department store. He loved the feel of his toes in cashmere socks.

He squeezed a dollop of body wash on his washcloth, working it until he got the foaming soapy suds he was after. He washed from head to toe, then used his hands to get in between, up, and under the places he wanted to smell the freshest. When he was done, he grabbed his shampoo and started on his hair. His hair was his favorite part of his body. It was big, black, sprinkled with a few grays, and full of unruly kinks, kind of like him. When his fro was picked out just right, it kept people away from him. He didn't like strangers and hated meaningless small talk even more. If someone ventured into his space with deep conversation and thought-provoking ideas, he tried his best to keep them in his life, which was why his circle was so small. With a head full of shampoo-silked hair, Dizzy grabbed his face wash and the small brush he used with it. His sensitive skin reacted badly to most soaps, so once he found one that left him clean, blemish-free, and highlighted his brown skin the color of dark Karo syrup, he bought it in bulk and never went anywhere overnight without it.

With his towel tucked low around his waist and a tee-shirt wrapped around his hair, Dizzy walked around his kitchen, phone in hand, listening to voicemails, checking emails, and replying to people who thought poor planning on their part constituted an emergency on his part. Along with writing for Dual Travel, he did some editing on the side. He loved writing for the magazine but wanted a more meaningful position, one that offered more interesting and personal stories. Stories with deeper feelings within his typed words.

An email from Shannon made him laugh. The URGENT in the subject line was an exaggeration. It was her trying to stay one step ahead of their boss, Ms. Hines. Cheryl Hines had owned Dual Travel for over twenty-five years. She'd gotten it from her husband in the divorce because he didn't think she could do anything with it. To his surprise, a few months later, it was selling off the shelves and doing better than even she knew it would. Shannon's email demanded he be at a meeting at one. Dizzy checked the clock to see it was only ten in the morning, but looking down, he was still in his towel with wet hair.

He tapped on the small curved arrow to reply, but Shannon's face popped up before he could start typing. "Hello, Shannon."

"Dizzy," she huffed out, sounding like she was power-walking through the hallway. He could hear the heels of her sensible shoes click-clacking on the floor. "You never answered my email."

"I just read it. What's going on, Shannon?"

"I can't tell you over the phone. I have to make sure you get here on time. Both of our jobs depend on it."

Dizzy knew the high-strung assistant was good with the dramatics, but he'd never heard his job leveraged as a way to get him to a meeting. "Is it that serious?" He picked up his sandwich and took a big bite, not bothering to swallow before he continued. "Is this a department thing or a Dizzy thing? I'm not rushing over there to be set up for bad news." He took another bite then washed it down with apple juice.

"It'll be you, Faye, and the Stuarts. Will you be there?"

"Yeah, I'll be there. See you at one."

CHAPTER 3

Five years ago

Faye stopped in front of the gleaming glass doors and smiled. She adjusted the strap on her brand-new purple leather satchel, a gift to herself for landing the writing position at Dual Travel. She was equally nervous and excited about walking through those doors for the first time as a staff member. She'd read every issue for the past three years, loving all the articles and their two perspectives, written by a team of two writers. Her favorite issue featured a small resort in Trinidad, and she brought up the picturesque memory in her mind of the sunny beaches and travelers in bikinis frolicking in the warm water as she stood outside in the January wind. Even though the chilly wind whipped around her, breezing through her recently big-chopped hair, she didn't let it rush her inside before her nerves were ready.

"You going in?" a man standing next to her asked. She didn't know how long he'd been there.

She'd been blissfully unaware in her excited nervousness. He motioned with his hand toward the long handle, then Faye finally spoke. "I am. Just...in a minute." The smile she gave him was both forced and awkward. "Go on in."

He looked around at all the passing pedestrians on the sidewalk and placed his hands to his sides. "How about I wait out here with you? I'm Dizzy." He stuck out his hand and waited for her to acknowledge his greeting.

"Faye." Even with the cold temperature, she could feel the warmth of his hand through her wool glove. "Do you work in this building?"

"Today's my first day. I'm writing for Dual Travel." The look of shock on her face made him laugh. "What? Don't like the magazine? Travel?"

No longer nervous, she answered, with a big smile, "I'm writing for them too."

"Well, Faye, how 'bout we go inside, get out of this wind, and start our first day?" Dizzy held his hands out toward the door, indicating he was waiting for her to make the first move. Feeling better she wasn't alone, Faye took a step forward toward the door. Joining her, Dizzy pulled the handle, and they walked in together.

"Hold the elevator!" Dizzy yelled, jogging up to the closing metal door. A hand swiped down the center, and he stepped in to see Faye leaning up against the wall. Her satchel was slung over her shoulder, and those lines in her forehead were prominent, showing her worry. "Hey, Shannon said you'd be here." Pressing the button three times for their floor, Dizzy stealthily looked Faye over. Her signature floral was a blouse showing off her strong arms. The skirt she wore showed off enough to be frustrating, but not enough to be suggestive. Faye was very mindful of what clothes she wore and how they fit her voluptuous body. In the five years he'd known her, she'd never dressed down or looked like she just rolled out of bed. Even her hair, today a side-swept afro with opal jewels contrasting against her black hair, was done with purpose, and he was sure it took forever, even though she made it look effortless. "You know what this is about?"

"No," she said worriedly. "The last time there was an emergency meeting, half of us got fired." She sighed, watching the numbered circles on the wall panel light up as the elevator rose.

"I don't think it's serious. It's probably nothing." Or so he hoped. He wanted to put Faye at ease. He never liked her worrying. "You alright?" She answered with a shallow nod before the elevator stopped and the doors opened. Dizzy waited for Faye to get off first, then followed her down the hall into the large conference room outfitted with an extra-long oval table that sat at least thirty but never had more than five people at a time at it.

The Stuarts were already seated when they walked in, looking like the quintessential happy Black couple. They had a storybook romance they loved to tell everyone about. One morning on her way to work, Tiffany rear-ended Kenny while putting on her mascara, and that was all it took. He was so mesmerized by her beauty, instead of taking her insurance information, he took her phone number, and they were married three months later. Faye had heard the tale so many times she'd stopped pretending it was a cute story. She didn't smile through it anymore, keeping her face blank as she counted the seconds it took Tiffany to throw her head back and laugh as Kenny joked about it. She would grab his arm and say, "Oh, honey, it wasn't that bad." They had perfected their routine. It was nauseating.

"Hey, guys, glad you could make it," Tiffany said, swaying side to side in her rolling chair. Kenny gave his customary head nod but didn't say anything. He left his greetings for their boss and strangers. "Did Shannon tell you what this is about?"

Dizzy pulled out Faye's chair before answering, "No. Just said to be here."

"Oh, good," Shannon said, whizzing by all of them. "You're all here." She went to the small fridge in the back of the room, grabbed some waters, and passed them out to everyone.

"Shannon," Kenny groaned. "Can you grab me another one? From the back. This one's not cold enough." Kenny held out his arm, holding the water bottle, shaking it when Shannon didn't get to him fast enough. "Today."

Exhaling, Shannon replaced Kenny's water then checked the thermostat on the wall and the roll of the chair at the head of the table, making sure it was Cheryl Hines-worthy. "Ms. Hines will be in here shortly." With a smile toward Dizzy and Faye, she hurried out of the room, leaving them all wondering what was going on.

It took ten minutes for Cheryl to glide into the room, wearing her ever-present black business suit and red-bottomed stilettos. No one knew her age because her penny-colored skin and honey blonde hair hid it well. She smiled when she looked out at them from the head of the table then sat, placing the portfolio she carried in with her flat on the table.

"Thank you for coming. This won't take long, but I wanted to give each of you time to prepare. "

Leaning into the table, moving the water bottle out of his way, Kenny asked, "Prepare for what?" His chest moved up and down as he breathed in and out.

"Your new assignments," she answered, smiling at each one of them before she opened her portfolio. She pulled out a stack of brochures, sliding them down the table. "As you know, our sales have seen a bit of a slump, and in order to recover as well as stay relevant and compete with the other magazines, we have to do something different."

"Union on Fire," Tiffany said, reading the brochure in her hand. "You're sending us on a retreat? Sounds fun." She looked at her husband, who looked skeptical because Cheryl never did anything nice for anyone. She was all business, especially when it came to her business.

"There's actually two different retreats," Cheryl said, holding up a glossy white trifold brochure. "Tiffany and Kenny, I'm sending you on a marriage retreat since you two are the only married couple at Dual Travel." Turning to Faye and Dizzy, she replaced the white brochure with one covered in green camo print. "You two get to go to the Survivalist Boot Camp."

Faye looked through the brochure again, making sure to read through all the words and examine each square picture thoroughly. "Is this like one of those doomsday places? They teach you how to survive if the world was to ever collapse, right?"

Cheryl pulled down her suit jacket and was about to speak when Dizzy cut her off.

"We're supposed to learn how to survive the end of the world?"

"It's what the brochure says," Cheryl confirmed. "You all know we have to do something no other publications are doing. 80% of our readership are women. They love things that will bring their marriage to new heights." Placing her hands on the table, Cheryl looked between Faye and Dizzy. "The other 20% are men who would rather be doing anything other than getting closer to their wives." They all turned to Kenny, who grunted. "Men love this prepper shit. The outdoors, hunter-gatherer type will eat this up. Sorry, Faye." She shrugged her shoulders, indicating Faye had no choice in the matter.

"Better her than me," Kenny spat out.

"It's only for two weeks. That shouldn't be too much to handle."

"Two weeks!" the four of them shouted together.

"I'm not sure about fourteen days, Cheryl." Kenny set his brochure face down on the table and folded his arms against his chest. Leaning back in his chair, he asked, "What's wrong with one week? It says it has a weeklong program." Tiffany's face fell a bit at her husband trying to cut a luxury marriage retreat in half.

"It does," Cheryl confirmed. "The more intense program is fourteen days. We want to give our readers the full experience, don't we?" She looked down at the table then back up, rolling her shoulders. "To stay in this race, we have to do what others aren't. So, fourteen days, it is."

She went on to talk about how, like times before, each of them would be responsible for writing an article about their personal experiences at their retreat. One of the ways Dual Travel was different from other publications was it gave at least two different perspectives when covering a story. Readers appreciated the way a married woman experienced the same thing a single man did and the different ways they wrote about them. This wasn't either of their first times working together. Tiffany and Kenny worked together exclusively and had quite a large fan base. The articles they wrote were always upbeat and cheery like them.

Working with Dizzy wasn't a problem for Faye. She actually preferred him to any of the other writers she'd been paired with in the past. Their backgrounds were different, but she got along with him better than anyone else.

"Look, I know it might be a little inconvenient, but if I need to find more writers, I will. I just want the story," Cheryl huffed out. She was getting that look of boredom and annoyance in her eyes. "I can find two other people to go to this marriage retreat." She looked directly at Kenny, who seemed the most put out by the assignment. "I can get people to pretend to be married for fourteen days if I need to."

"We're good, Cheryl," Tiffany said with a small smile, touching Kenny's hand. "It's not a problem. We look forward to it."

Kenny spoke up, scratching his eyebrow with his thumb. "Spending a couple of weeks in luxury while they play in the mud and learn which leaves are best to wipe with sounds like fun."

"Good." Cheryl smiled, pleased, even though she could tell Kenny wasn't 100% convinced. "And to make things more interesting, the team with the best story gets it featured on the cover. Good luck."

CHAPTER 4

"**D**id the brochure say what we needed to get? I'm not trying to go broke learning how to survive the end of the world." Faye buckled her seatbelt and waited for Dizzy to get in on the other side of his truck to answer her question.

He'd called last night so they could go shopping for the boot camp gear, saying he figured she might not have the right clothes for the hiking and horseback riding the pictures showed. "There was a small list on the back, but nothing surprising. They provide tents, but not much else," he answered after he closed the door. "I think we'll be able to find everything in one trip." He pulled out into the street, adjusting the vent to make sure she got air. "The pictures looked nice, but you can never be too prepared when it comes to the apocalypse."

The ride to the store didn't hold much conversation. Faye sang along to the songs on the radio the whole way. Dizzy learned a long time ago that when Faye was in the car, it was best to stay quiet while she belted out song after song as close to in tune as she could get. She refused to use Bluetooth, insisting a playlist was too structured. She liked the freedom the radio allowed. Never knowing what the next song was going to be was part of the fun for her, even if she flipped through all twenty of the preset stations Dizzy had allowed her to program. She always skipped over the sports talk stations he was adamant she set when she programmed them almost two years ago.

The first time she rode with him, Faye immediately went for the buttons on the dash to change the station. She gave him a beautiful wide grin to stop him from complaining, and it had been that way ever since. She would sing along to a few bars of a song Dizzy had never heard, then she'd press another button on the dash to bring up a new station—she had no patience for commercials.

"Why do you always do that?" Dizzy asked after she switched stations mid-song.

"Do what?" She bopped in her seat to the music as they pulled into the parking lot, looking for the perfect space not too far from the entrance or too close for someone to ding Dizzy's truck with their door.

"Change the station while you're in the middle of singing a song." He pulled into the spot and waited for Faye to finish harmonizing with Whitney Houston before turning off the car. "You're a piece of work, you know?"

She smiled at him. "I know," Faye said, stepping out of the truck. "Who wants to be tied down to a song when you don't have to be?" Dizzy placed his hand at the small of her back to nudge her out of the way of a wayward child pushing an oversized cart. She lost her train of thought.

"You were saying?"

"Um—" Faye exhaled. She was sure Dizzy, always the gentleman, had touched her on the small of her back before. This was the first time she ever felt it.

"Tell me more about these songs you only like listening to

halfway through."

She pressed her lips together, then thought about how she wanted to answer his question. She equated listening to music to dating, but she wasn't sure she wanted to explain or if he'd even understand her reasoning.

Faye liked dating—or the idea of dating, the exhilaration of getting dressed up and going someplace nice for great conversation and a few laughs. When she was in her twenties, she stayed on dates. Every Friday and Saturday, she was getting dressed up to be wined and dined, sometimes more than once. A brunch date with one guy then a dinner date with a different guy wasn't unheard of for Faye. That was the problem Francine had. She didn't understand why Faye, at the age of forty, was still dating. She couldn't fathom that she didn't want to settle for the first man who showed a little bit of interest. For Faye to make a date with several men went against everything Francine had been taught. It irked her to no end to know her daughter was out with yet another man as if she hadn't had a date with someone else a few nights ago. What Faye could never make her accept was that the dates were just that. They'd meet somewhere, talk, eat, laugh, but that was as far as it got. She hadn't felt the need to exclusively date anyone in almost a decade. No one seemed worth the trouble. Faye wasn't one to beat a dead horse. She usually knew after the first hour that the date wouldn't turn into anything romantic. She was always looking for that spark, those flutters in her chest telling her she was in front of the One. All she'd gotten in the past were fizzles.

"If you have five three-minute songs you like, why not listen to them at the same time or back-to-back without any interruptions? It's more exciting that way. Why suffer through the lull of the last long note when it gets boring? No one wants that."

No matter how many dates her mother tried to set her up on, Faye was never interested in the men Francine wanted her to be with. They were stuffy and pretentious and too concerned with keeping up with the Joneses even though they were the Joneses. None of them were worth messing up her lipstick for.

"I can understand that," Dizzy said, following Faye down the aisle to the backpacks. "I've definitely been bored by a few songs that seemed to never end."

Forty-five minutes later, they had a cart full of stuff Dizzy insisted they'd need for the end of the world, including new swim trunks because you never know when you might have to swim your way out of danger.

"You think we'd have time to change into these?" Faye held up an all-black one-piece that would look great on any Olympic swimmer but wasn't even close to her style. "I know you're chasing me, Mr. Monster, but please let me slip on my sleek bathing suit before you grab me," she teased.

Dizzy didn't laugh. Instead, he took it from her and hung it back on the rack. "It matches mine, though." Dizzy's lime green and white polka-dotted swim trunks he'd picked out ten minutes ago were the last pair long enough for his tall frame. He'd thrown them in the basket, excited for the find.

"So, we need to match?"

"Teamwork and solidarity, right?" Dizzy asked. His eyebrow quirked at the way Faye bit the inside of her cheek, trying not to laugh. "We'll look good when we win."

"You can't win the end of the world, Dizzy." He shrugged, disputing her claim. They already had matching cargo pants and denim shirts. Dizzy told her the denim was tough enough to get them through the most grueling challenges. Add them to the tee-shirts, extra-thick socks, and ace bandages, and they were almost ready to leave.

"Depending on what the prize is, I most definitely would win the end of the world." His stare caught her off guard. "And no, living isn't the prize." He shook his head, continuing to walk them down another aisle. "You have to have something to live for."

Faye nodded, understanding. "Winning the end of the world seems like the best prize. A lonely prize, but the ultimate prize." Dizzy pressed his lips together and nodded at Faye in agreement. "I can get with that," Faye said. The look he gave her was endearing, and Faye turned her head to redirect her focus.

Dizzy had always been one who fought hard for what he wanted, your classic country boy. He moved to the city after graduating from college to be close to available jobs, but his heart was always on the family farm. "You know what we should get you?" Dizzy asked, looking down at the glass case in front of him. He didn't wait for an answer. "A knife."

"What am I supposed to do with a knife? You think they'll teach us how to clean fish?"

Dizzy tapped on the glass, indicating which one he wanted Faye to see. "I already know how to do all that. I was thinking more about protection." Faye leaned her elbow on the counter to look at him while he finished talking. "What if I'm not around? These survivor places have some weird people who go to them. We might be going for a story, but for them, it's real life."

Faye thought his concern was sweet. She'd never thought about carrying a weapon outside of her taser she kept on her keyring, but she could see his point. "Okay, which one should I get?"

"I like this one." Dizzy pointed again to the one he was

looking at, then motioned with his head for the salesperson.
"You have to decide, though. Find the one that feels the best in
your hand."

Faye nodded, then took the knife the salesperson handed
her. She tried six knives, spring-loaded and folded, finally
deciding on a small spring-loaded tactical knife because she
liked the finger grooves and how fast the blade came out. Dizzy
approved, impressed with the way she handled it. "I like this
one," Faye said to the salesperson. "But I hate this color." She
could see Dizzy shaking his head out of the corner of her eye.
"Does it come in floral?"

CHAPTER 5

Years of travel had taught Dizzy the best way to pack a suitcase, but stuffing a backpack full of two weeks' worth of clothes and gear was something new to him. It had been a feat he didn't think he'd ever figure out, but around two in the morning, he was able to get everything he needed into the canvas bag.

A few hours later, at 6:45, he rolled over and turned off the alarm on his phone. He hadn't been up this excited in years. He hadn't traveled out of town in a while. He needed a change of scenery, and two weeks with Faye was the best part.

Cheryl made it clear everyone needed to be at Dual Travel by 8 a.m. He had enough time to shower, put something in his belly, and pick up Faye before Shannon started angrily texting through all caps and three too many exclamation points.

Backing into the parking space closest to Faye's apartment, Dizzy noticed he was one of the few out at the early weekend time. Even the birds seemed to be chirping in whispers to allow people to sleep in a bit longer. He knocked three times on Faye's door, and, "Be right there," came almost immediately. It took about ninety seconds for her door to open, with Faye walking away to allow him to enter on his own.

"Come in. I'm running late." She was adjusting the earring in her ear from what he could see as she walked further away from him. "You want some coffee? I've got Styrofoam if you want to take it with you." Her voice trailed off as she got further away from him, walking to her room.

He laughed to himself because he'd never seen Faye not ready. She was the one you could set your clock to. "You doing alright?" he asked, closing the door behind him.

"Yeah, just...kind of nervous." She came back out with a pink v-neck shirt tucked into her black cargos. He felt his heart falter, not remembering them fitting that way at the store. She finished the look in true Faye fashion with a pink floral belt around her waist. Dizzy could hear her rummaging through her room, opening and closing drawers. When the noise stopped, Faye hopped back into the living room, trying to get her hiking boots on. "First, I couldn't decide what to pack, so I was up way past midnight. Then I couldn't sleep. I dreamt we were chased by zombies."

Dizzy laughed, relieved he wasn't the only one who couldn't sleep. "Did we get away?"

"I don't know," she answered, making sure her laces were tight enough. "Out of nowhere, a giant squirrel was there, and then my alarm went off."

"I hope you don't have those kinds of dreams in the tent," Dizzy laughed, walking toward the kitchen. "You want coffee?"

"Yes."

Dizzy looked back but didn't see her. "Where'd you go?" The pot was full when he reached for it. He heard her mumble something from her room but didn't ask her to repeat it. He poured a cup for himself, then a bigger one for Faye. He was dumping the second spoonful of sugar into her mug when she came back.

"How many is that?"

"Two," he answered, holding the spoon between her mug and the sugar. "How many more you need?" She held up two fingers, and Dizzy complied, dropping the spoon in the mug so Faye could stir. "You got everything?"

Faye licked the coffee off the spoon then tossed it into the sink. "Yep." She raised her mug then took a sip. "Thank you." Dizzy watched her close her eyes and savor the flavor and the jolt of caffeine as it entered her body. He took a moment to study her face, the thickness of her eyebrows, the slight flare of her nostrils as she breathed out after she swallowed. "Do you think we'll be able to handle two weeks in the wilderness?"

Growing up on a farm, being outdoors wasn't a problem for Dizzy. He was used to all of it. He wasn't certain Faye could, but he knew she wouldn't give up or quit on him. She dressed the part of the prissy princess, but she was tough as nails when she needed to be. "I think we'll do just fine," he answered.

She'd been practicing her army crawl and even ate out of a can the other night in preparation for the boot camp, but she knew one meal didn't make her ready. "For two weeks?" She had a frown that showed she'd added up exactly how many minutes made up those two weeks. He already knew he was going to enjoy each and every one of his 20, 160 minutes with her.

"We'll take it day by day," Dizzy said, finishing his coffee. He washed out his mug and the spoon Faye tossed in the sink earlier. "We gotta head out before Shannon starts blowing up our phones." He held his hand out for her mug, then waited for her to gulp the coffee down quickly before handing it to him.

"Fine, day by day, it is," Faye said. "I better come out of this stronger, smarter, and knowing how to use that tactical knife you made me buy."

"Oh my God, where have you two been?" The constantly frantic Shannon met them at the front of the building, clipboard in one hand, phone in the other. She was unusually dressed down in a vintage Purple Rain tee-shirt and jeans. Her normally perfectly coiled hair was under a plain black cap hiding her frustrated face. "Didn't you get my messages? You should have been here —" she looked down at her watch and tapped the screen to check the time "—six minutes ago. We're on a very tight schedule."

"Good morning, Shannon," Faye said, ignoring her frantic hand gestures. "Is the car here so we can put our stuff in?" Faye adjusted the strap on her backpack, her back already killing her from the weight.

"Keep it on you, the cars should be here any minute now. Ms. Hines is expecting both of you upstairs. There's more paperwork to sign, and she wants to talk to you privately, Dizzy." Shannon looked around both of them to the street and the cars she was expecting. When she didn't say anything else, they walked away, leaving her standing there looking at her watch and tapping her pen on her clipboard.

As the elevator doors opened to their floor, Dizzy saw Kenny first in the hallway, then Tiffany squatting down, checking the contents of one of the many bags she had with her. The posh marital retreat they were going to appeared really relaxing and cozy from the pictures Tiffany showed them. It was apparent they were overprepared by all the luggage they had. Kenny gave Dizzy a head nod, then pointed in the direction of the conference room where Cheryl was most likely waiting.

"Finally," Cheryl said when they walked into the room. She, too, was dressed down, at least for her. She wore a fitted black tee-shirt and black jeans with shiny black Louis Vuitton heels. "There's a few more papers we need signed. One is regarding the rental car and liability. It's on the top." She pointed at two stacks of papers on the table, each with a Dual Travel pen on top. Dizzy pulled out Faye's chair, and they skimmed the paperwork. They'd signed this same stack twenty times before. With multiple trips behind them, neither bothered reading through the seven pieces of paper. They signed or initialed wherever they saw a neon sticky note arrow. When they were done, they pushed the stacks away and stood up, ready to get into survival mode.

"Is that it?" Faye asked

"That's all I need," Cheryl answered. "Faye, head on downstairs while I talk to Dizzy for a bit. The cars should be here by now. Shannon probably wants to take inventory of what all you're taking before you drive away." She looked at Faye and gave her a fake smile. "Have a good time, hon."

She went to grab her backpack, but Dizzy stopped her. "I got it. Go calm Shannon down before she starts screaming up from the street."

When Faye got downstairs, Shannon was crawling into a black SUV while Kenny stood on the sidewalk waiting for the all-clear. "Where's Tiffany?" Faye asked, looking around at the passing traffic. She stretched her back, working out the tension. No amount of yoga had prepared her for carrying around the weight of a stuffed backpack full of survival gear for the end of the world.

"She had to run back upstairs for something," he answered,

scanning the area around Faye. "I know y'all are going to be roughing it for a bit, but don't you think you should at least bring something?"

"Dizzy has my bag." The five bags at Kenny's feet seemed excessive, but she didn't say anything. She might be the same way if she had the chance to be pampered for two weeks in a room with walls and a place to pee that didn't involve nature.

Kenny looked her over, lingering on her hiking boots for longer than was necessary, then moved his eyes up to the cornrows in her hair. "You think you're gonna make it the whole fourteen days?" Faye had never really liked Kenny. He gave off vibes that weren't genuine enough for her. He smiled at her, then pulled out his phone, dismissing her and ending the conversation before she answered his question.

Shannon crawled backward out of the SUV on her hands and knees, wiping her hands off on her jeans when she stood up. She looked pleased, her eyes brighter than they were when Faye and Dizzy first arrived. "Looks like everything's in order for your trip, Kenny." He didn't respond as he scrolled through his phone. She drew three authoritative checks on her clipboard then mumbled, "Just need to get y'all on the road. Um, here." She shoved a piece of paper in his face. "Fill these out, so we know what you're taking of value if anything gets lost or stolen."

"We know, Shannon," he groaned.

With a sinister smile that Kenny didn't see, she asked, "Where's Dizzy and Tiffany?"

"I'm here," Tiffany announced, exiting the building loaded down with bags. She drew in a deep breath. "Dizzy's still talking to Cheryl." She gave Kenny a look Faye assumed was some secret married couple code for something only they cared about. "Can we start loading up?"

"Yes," Shannon said happily. "There's a full tank of gas,

which should be enough to get you there and back. I put a
basket of snacks and bottles of water on the middle row. Please
don't make a mess; the cleaner we return the van, the better. All
the numbers you'll need for roadside assistance are in the glove
box, and if you happen to, I don't know, hit a deer or brake too
hard for a raccoon, please call the rental company first."

Kenny opened the hatch at the back to start loading their
bags in. He and Tiffany had a total of seven bags and suitcases
between them. She couldn't imagine what was in them. By the
look of some, they'd planned new outfits for each meal.

"You get some new clothes, Faye?" Tiffany asked, handing a
bag to Kenny. They were both dressed more casual than usual,
but the jeans and blue flowy-sleeve shirt Tiffany wore was a lot
dressier than the tee-shirt Faye wore. "Are those cargo pants?"

"Finally!" Shannon exclaimed, looking at Dizzy joining the
group. "They'll fill you in on what I told them about the
paperwork." She looked down at her phone. "You have ten
minutes to get on the road." She opened the driver's side door
to the car Dizzy and Faye would be taking. The silver sedan
seemed roomy enough for both their long legs, but it was a lot
smaller than the truck Dizzy was used to driving.

"Hiking boots, really?" Tiffany looked from Faye to Dizzy's
feet. "Oh, look, Kenny, they're both wearing boots. How sweet."
Kenny shut the hatch, then looked down at Dizzy's feet in his
signature cowboy boots. He shook his head, chuckled, then
walked to the driver's side to get in.

"Tiffany, you and Kenny need to leave now," Shannon
shouted out from the backseat of Dizzy and Faye's car. She was
still inspecting the rental, hoping she found something to write
down.

"Well, I guess we'll see you two in two weeks." Tiffany
looked over at the back of the SUV and the taillights when

Kenny started the car. "Enjoy the wilderness." She walked off and sat next to Kenny. They drove away five minutes later.

"Okay. Looks like you're all set," Shannon said, bouncing out of the car. She drew three more checks on her clipboard, then took the papers they had in their hands.

"What will you do without us for two weeks, Shannon?" Dizzy asked, watching Shannon's face light up.

"With Cheryl out of the office, I'm going on vacation."

"Anywhere special?" Faye asked.

Looking down at her watch, Shannon grinned and nodded. "My brand-new mattress that was delivered yesterday and a bunch of Netflix movies I haven't had time to watch yet."

"Enjoy your me-time, girl," Faye said, watching Dizzy load the bags into the trunk.

"We'll see you when we get back," Dizzy said, opening Faye's door. They both waved to Shannon as she stood on the sidewalk, watching them drive away.

CHAPTER 6

An hour later, Faye turned off the radio. The spotty reception kept it at a constant state of static, so she couldn't enjoy the ride like she was used to. Luckily, Dizzy filled the silence by talking to her about his plans and keeping her talking by asking her thoughts.

"So, you'd travel the country interviewing farmers?"

"Black farmers," Dizzy corrected. "Yeah, I've been thinking about it for a while. It's time I put some miles on my truck, some clicks on my camera." He told her more about his family's farm and how his dad used to tell stories about farmer meetings where the room was full of Black farmers. Through the years, the numbers dwindled as the farmers lost their land to shady USDA practices steeped in racism. "What do you think?" Dizzy asked Faye, looking at her as he drove before turning his eyes to the road again.

"Sounds like what you were made for, Dizzy." His plan was solid, and she knew he could do it. She was happy for him, but something inside her felt sad, knowing he wouldn't be there for her to look at from across their office. "I can't wait to read it." It was quiet for a bit as they both sat with their thoughts. Hoping to cut some of the somberness of the trip, Faye asked, "You gonna be alright not talking to Billie for two weeks?" She hoped he took it as a joke but knew how much his niece meant to him. "How did she take the news you'd be gone?"

"It's not like I've never been away from her." He looked over at Faye, who was holding in her laugh. She could tell he missed her already. "I had to say 'boot camp' three times for her to get it. She kept calling it 'booty camp.'" They both laughed, imagining what a booty camp would involve. Once he could speak again, Dizzy continued, "She seemed fine after I told her I needed her to look after Miles and Cecily."

"I bet she didn't hear anything about your trip after that."

"She did not," he agreed, shaking his head. "She's something else."

Dizzy's relationship with Billie had always made Faye smile. He wore his heart on his sleeve, and when it came to Billie, his love for her radiated from the inside out. She had him wrapped around her finger, and he knew it. It was one of his most endearing qualities. She patted his hand, resting on his knee. "You'll be alright." She felt him laugh then looked at him as he refocused on the road. Giving his hand a small squeeze, she let go and watched the trees as they passed by.

"Um, Dizzy, this looks nothing like the brochure. Are you sure this is the right place?" Faye asked, looking around at all the cars being directed to drive up to a huge circular driveway. "Shit, I left the brochure in my backpack. I don't remember seeing a big mansion in any of the pictures."

"Everything's probably in the back. This has to be

registration or something." He crept along slowly, following the cars ahead of him, looking around at the perfectly trimmed bushes and the evenly paved driveway. They both jumped when Faye's door was opened.

"Welcome to the Union on Fire retreat," the peppy man who'd opened the door said. He took a quick look around the inside of the car, then said, "If your luggage is in the trunk, grab what you can carry, and the rest, you can put these tags on, and we'll bring them in for you."

Dizzy looked at Faye, both confused. They both mouthed, 'Union on Fire,' to each other, then Dizzy's door was opened. He stepped out in a daze, followed by Faye, meeting at the trunk as it popped open.

"This isn't where we're supposed to be," Faye whispered. All the activity and movement around them drowned out her voice, but she was too shocked to speak louder. "The Stuarts had this place." She looked around again, taking in all the people walking to the front door. "None of these people are dressed for an apocalypse, Dizzy."

He bounced a little to get his backpack in place, then grabbed hers and took her by the arm to lead her to the front doors. "Yeah, well, maybe Shannon gave us the wrong directions. I'm sure it's an easy fix, we'll call—" They'd left their phones at Faye's, wanting to get the full survivalist experience by not relying on technology. "Shit," Dizzy uttered as Faye nodded.

A woman standing near the entrance spoke and smiled. Shocked, Faye didn't hear what she'd said. She was dressed in a crisp white polo with the collar turned upward. The letters *UF* were embroidered in bright yellow thread across her left chest. The braids she wore hung low, down to her waist, and were decorated with yellow, white, and black beads. Faye made eye contact, and the woman motioned with her hand for them to go inside. Still being led by Dizzy, she blinked, not believing what was happening.

"Welcome. Follow the arrows on the floor, they'll lead you to the registration table. It's by last name, so make sure you're in the right line." The voice from a bullhorn repeated the instructions a few more times before going silent.

"We'll tell them at the registration table we're in the wrong place," Dizzy said low enough for Faye to hear. "Our names aren't on the list, anyway. They'll figure it out."

Without their names on the list, there's no way they could stay, Faye thought. "Okay," she said, feeling better. "Uh, let's go this way." She pulled Dizzy by the hand toward the R-T table. "We'll have them look up the Stuarts' name and then tell them about the mix-up."

"Hello, welcome to Union on Fire. Can I get your name, please?" the chipper woman behind the red-clothed table asked, smiling big, showing off her perfect white teeth.

"Stuart. Tiffany and Kenny Stuart." Faye looked smugly at Dizzy, knowing this would work and get them where they were supposed to be, at the end of the world. She watched the woman scroll down her list with the tip of her pen, then flip the page. She did the same thing down five pages before looking up perplexed, but still with a smile.

"I'm sorry, I don't have any Stuarts on the list. Are you sure that was the name the reservation was placed under?"

"Yes, there's no other name."

"I'm sorry. I don't have that name listed." Smiling, she placed her pen down and crossed her arms in front of her on the table. "Try the office. It's to the left of the front entrance. Maybe there was an issue with your paperwork or something."

"Paula, is there a problem?" A short, bald man walked up,

holding a tablet, looking over the rims of his glasses.

"Mr. Kelly, these two don't appear to be on my list. I was just directing them to your office to get things sorted out."

His eyes darted from the woman named Paula to Dizzy, then Faye. His stubby fingers stabbed at the tablet screen, then he swiped and typed something. The brightness of the screen lit up his face. "I'm sure we can get this all sorted out. Now, what did you say your name was?"

"Kenny Stuart," Dizzy answered, hesitantly.

Mr. Kelly typed in the name, then swiped the screen a few times. He shook his head from side to side. "Did you make the reservation?"

Faye dropped her head to Dizzy's arm, allowing him to answer while she sorted through the ways this had gone wrong. She was supposed to be learning how to build bunkers and can squirrel meat. "No," Dizzy said. "Uh, our job, Dual Travel, made it. Maybe you have something under the name Shannon Porter."

"Porter, Porter." Mr. Kelly said, then smiled. "Ah, yes. Shannon Porter with Dual Travel. Reservations for Dizzy Freeman and Faye Morris. Is that not you?" He looked over his glasses again.

Faye lifted her head, her forehead wrinkled in confusion. "That's us, but we—"

"Problem solved, then. Just head to the correct table, and we'll get you checked in."

He walked away, leaving Dizzy and Faye more confused than before. Paula waved the people standing behind them to her, and to Faye's dismay, everyone went on as if nothing was going on.

"Dizzy, why are we registered to be here?"

"Don't know, Faye."

Taking the steps to the D-F table, Faye could feel her heart catch up with her brain. Not only were they at the wrong place, but they were also at a retreat focused on marriage. She'd spent all week getting her mind ready for surviving in the wilderness, learning how to be the last one standing when the world ended. She'd even set her misgivings aside and decided if she needed to trap a squirrel or catch fish with her bare hands, she would. She was ready to win.

"Here you go, Mr. and Mrs. Freeman. Your room is on the right. The valets will bring the rest of your luggage to your room shortly." The unfamiliar voice brought Faye halfway out of her haze. She didn't remember walking up to the table or even if she spoke to whoever had talked to them. Now, apparently, she had forgotten how to walk because Dizzy was leading her by the arm in the direction of their room.

The click of the door lock after Dizzy inserted the key card brought her back fully. She focused on the silver handle as it moved away from her as Dizzy pushed the door open and held it, waiting for her to walk through.

Closing her eyes, she took one deep breath before stepping over the threshold, then gasped when her eyes opened, and she saw the huge pristine room that would be theirs for fourteen days. "Wow," she gushed, walking further in. The oversized suite with its large living area had a huge cream-colored sectional with a large TV on one side and an intimate dining area on the other. Dizzy dropped their bags down and scanned the room, too, impressed with what he saw. Faye walked to a pair of sliding glass doors leading outside.

Dizzy whistled low and long, looking at the space. "This is a lot nicer than sleeping in a tent."

Faye stared out to the lush greenness outside, then opened the door and stepped out. "There's a hot tub and a hammock out here, Dizzy." She smiled for the first time since stepping into the resort. "I might not leave!"

"So, you're alright with this?"

The concern on his face was reassuring since she knew he was worried about her reaction. "Dizzy, this is a five-star resort." She smiled and walked to him. This time, it was her turn to lead him. She walked him to the couch where they sat, sighing at how comfortable the cushions felt underneath them. "They have massages, room service, a huge-ass pool." The afternoon Tiffany showed her the brochure flooded Faye's memory. Tiffany had said something snide about how different the two assignments were, then shoved the glossy rectangle in her face. Faye had skimmed through the pictures, feeling jealous of the pretty green grass and clear blue water of the pool. "This is like the vacation we deserve, Dizzy." She took a breath, then let it out slowly. "I was trippin' when we first drove up, and we were in the wrong place, but like my Grandmother says, God don't make no mistakes. We deserve this."

"And the Stuarts?"

"Fuck them," she said with a laugh. "You grew up on a farm, you know how to survive. They need the practice."

Dizzy stood up, laughing, running his hand over his fro and looking at Faye. "You sure?"

"I mean, we don't have anything but what we brought in our backpacks, but I'm down if you are." She stuck her hand out to offer a handshake. "What do you say, husband?"

His smile grew, and he swiped his tongue across his bottom lip. "I'm in, Mrs. Freeman."

CHAPTER 7

Dizzy looked at Faye from across the room. Agreeing to play husband and wife seemed innocent enough when her hand was in his to make the deal. Neither of them thought the logistics through, though. Staring at the king-sized bed between the two of them now seemed like a problem. This was nothing like sharing a tent with individual sleeping bags as they planned. This was one single mattress, covered in a higher thread count sheet than either of them could afford, satin pillowcases, and a duvet that looked good enough to wrap up and sleep the week away in. Dizzy pressed down on the mattress, and his hand sank down.

"If you don't want to share, we can always arm wrestle for it." He could feel her trepidation from across the room. All her tough talk from half an hour ago disappeared as soon as they walked into the bedroom to see only one bed.

"No, no," Faye said, pacing the length of the bed, biting on her thumbnail. "This isn't a problem. Of course, there's one bed. It's a marriage retreat. This isn't an episode of I Love Lucy. Married people share beds all the time." Dizzy stayed quiet, allowing her to talk her way through it. This was part of her process of working through things she wasn't sure of. She stopped pacing, then sat down. "Holy shit, Dizzy. This is a lot." She wiggled her butt into the mattress, then bounced up and down. "It doesn't even make any noise." She groaned, lying back with a sigh, extending her arms to the side then moving them up and down like she was making a snow angel. "I don't mind sharing if you don't, but I'm not giving this bed up."

It wasn't the smell of eggs and syrup that woke Dizzy up, but the bright stream of light from the window and his arm being numb from sleeping on the couch. He'd thrown it over his eyes before he went to bed and woke up the same way. He sat up, squinting to let his eyes adjust, then looked toward the opened bedroom door. The empty bed was in view, but Faye was nowhere in sight. Last night, he'd told Faye he'd take the couch and let her enjoy the plush mattress by herself. Even with her demonstrating how a line of pillows down the middle of the bed could work so they'd both be able to sleep in it, Dizzy didn't want to take the chance, especially after Faye finished her shower and put on the thin nighty she'd found in the welcome basket. He'd taken a cooler than usual shower, then headed for the couch, taking one of the pillows with him.

The small dining table was loaded with food. The eggs he smelled were omelets filled with tomatoes and mushrooms, and the syrup in the pourer was still warm, ready to be drizzled over the strawberry and chocolate-filled crêpes. Dizzy wasted no time sampling a small bite of the sausage on the tray but left everything else in case Faye hadn't eaten. He poured a glass of juice then took it out to the back patio to get a glimpse of the grounds in the morning sun. He almost dropped it when he found Faye bent at the waist, her hands touching the ground and her right leg in the air, her foot almost touching her head in a yoga pose.

"Morn—" He cleared the sleep out of his voice. "Morning." His head involuntarily tilted to see her face and keep his eyes from roving the lines of her body as she posed in a position he'd never seen but was glad she'd been the one to show him.

"Hey." She gave him a quick smile, then looked to the ground again.

"What— what are you doing?"

"Three-legged downward dog. Want to try it?"

Dizzy shook his head even though she couldn't see him. "How long you been up?

She brought her leg down, then moved into a sun salutation before answering. "About an hour and a half. I woke up when they brought breakfast. You were knocked out, so I let you sleep." Breakfast was wheeled into the room as quietly as possible while Dizzy slept. Faye had ignored the questioning eyes of room service, who spotted Dizzy curled up on the couch. "Are you hungry? I wanted to wait until you were up before I dug in. Came out here, so I didn't have to smell the food." She sat down on the ground, putting her legs into a wide V to stretch, bringing her chest down to deepen the pose.

Dizzy swallowed hard, the juice in his throat suddenly feeling like cement on its way down. He looked out to the trees in the distance to focus on something safer. "I'm gonna brush my teeth. I'll meet you back inside." He turned on his heel, groaning silently at his reaction to Faye. His attraction wasn't new, but it was hitting him differently this morning. He prayed he could keep himself in check. This was day two. 18,711 minutes to go.

"So..." Faye speared a sausage with her fork, adding it to her already full plate. "I was thinking." Her mouth opened wide for the crêpe she was putting into it. "We didn't talk to many people yesterday, but according to that lady... What was her name, the one with the cute fade?"

"Sylvia," Dizzy answered, watching the syrup on Faye's top lip disappear when she licked it.

"Yeah, her. She said we're going on a nature hike as a group today. We need to get our story straight." She reached for a piece of strawberry that fell from her crêpe. "You know, the details couples should know about each other."

Dizzy added more salsa to his omelet, making sure it didn't mix with the syrup on the plate. "How long have we been married, Mrs. Freeman?" The omelet was made to perfection, and he took two big forkfuls waiting for Faye's answer.

She shrugged, taking a sip of her juice. "Let's go with five years. It's easy to remember." She reached over the table to get the fallen mushroom from Dizzy's omelet. "Where'd we meet?"

"Work," he answered. "It's the truth." He watched her nod, then used his fork to block her from coming back to get the rest of the omelet fillings on his plate. "Don't you have your own food?"

"My husband's food is always my food."

"Is that right?" Dizzy moved his fork and laughed, allowing her to get her fill from his plate. "What else should we know about each other?"

They spent the rest of their breakfast asking and answering questions they thought a couple should know about each other. Favorite food—Faye loved banana pudding, Dizzy, stew. Faye's favorite color was yellow, and Dizzy's was green. They knew everything about each other—years of working together left nothing unknown. The only question they stumbled on was the worst color M&M.

"They all taste the same, Dizzy," Faye said from the other

side of the bathroom door. She was jumping into her cargos for their hike. "It's just colored chocolate. You know that, right?"

Dizzy used the bedroom to get dressed and tried to get her to see his point. "No one likes blue ones. They taste different." He looked up when Faye came out of the bathroom wearing a yellow tee-shirt and another pair of black cargos. "Um." Dizzy ran his hand down his mustache, blowing out a breath. "They're —"

"They're all the same, Dizzy." She looked at her watch, then back at him. "We gotta hustle. Ten minutes until the morning meeting." She started putting on her hiking boots when there was a knock on the door.

"I'll get it." Dizzy tucked his shirt in on the way to the door, looking back at Faye to make sure she was decent.

"Oh, hey," a voice said before the door was opened fully. "I was wondering who our neighbors were." The woman behind the voice was short and had to crane her neck up to Dizzy and Faye, who'd joined him at the door. "I'm Regina, and my husband Thomas is—" she looked to her left then exhaled, rolling her eyes. "In the room. We're in fourteen, right there. Is this your first time?"

Dizzy looked to Faye, who spoke for both of them. "It's nice to meet you, Regina. I'm Faye." She reached to hold Dizzy's hand. "This is my husband, Dizzy." Dropping her hand, Dizzy wrapped his arm around her waist, squeezing her hip.

"Well, aren't y'all the cutest? And so tall." Her eyes traveled from Faye's shoes up to her waist. "Man, I wished my legs went up that high. How tall are you, honey?"

"Six feet, ma'am," Faye replied with a smile, starting to feel uncomfortable with the way Regina was gawking at her and Dizzy. She was used to people staring at her because of her height, but Regina seemed to be ogling her with a creepy smile on her face. Dizzy noticed, too, so when Faye started moving behind him, he made sure she was covered by his body.

"It was nice meeting you, Regina," Dizzy said, "but it looks like it's time to head to the common room." He felt Faye's warmth move from behind him, then saw her pick up the key card and slip it into her back pocket. "Time for the morning meeting."

Faye discreetly looked down at her watch, then back up at Steven, the retreat leader. They'd been in the common room for almost two hours listening to introductions, testimonials, and a quick rundown of the activities for the day. She yawned openly, tired of hiding them behind her hand.

"Thank y'all for hanging in with us," Steve said, rubbing his hands together. "I know we've been sitting for a bit. Right now, we're gonna take a short break, let y'all have a few refreshments, then we'll come back for our first exercise before you head off to the group activity."

"This is pretty wild, huh?" Justine asked Faye at the refreshments table. They'd met earlier when they sat down next to each other. It was her and her husband's second time at the boot camp. "I think I was in a daze last year. I'm focusing this year." She grabbed a banana off the table and started peeling. "Did you see the hot tub? Ugh! It's my favorite part of this whole place." She smiled big, then tugged on her shirt. "Plus, these clothes they give us. Everything fits so perfectly. Have you tried the big fluffy robe yet? Whenever I put it on, I fall asleep."

Faye sipped her drink and smiled politely, nodding her head, not sure what to respond to first. "I can't believe I'm here," she said. "It might take me a few days to get used to it all."

"Maybe a dip in your hot tub will help," Justine said.

"I got you some fruit before that greedy couple over there took it all," Dizzy's voice cut in. All three of them turned to a tall woman and her shorter husband, who both had a plate in each hand, piled high with two of everything.

"Dizzy, right?" Justine asked. He nodded his head to answer. She looked around the room, searching for her husband. "I don't think you met Russell before. He's in the red polo by the coffee." She pointed, and Russell looked up, giving her a smile. "He's no good unless he's had at least three cups."

Regina walked up to them, smiling, carrying a bottle of water. "Hope I'm not interrupting. I wanted to introduce my husband to y'all." She turned to her left but didn't see anyone. "Damn it, Thomas, over here." She motioned with her whole arm for him to come, then waited as he walked to them with a plate full of sandwich roll-ups. "Honey, this is Faye and Dizzy. The ones I was telling you about." She smiled in the direction of Justine.

"Oh, Regina," Faye spoke. "This is Justine. Her husband's over there drinking coffee."

"Nice to meet you," Justine said sweetly, showing off the cute gap between her teeth.

Regina nodded, then turned to Faye again. "Didn't I tell you she was pretty?" Regina asked Thomas. This time, without any prompting, Dizzy stepped in front of Faye to stop Thomas from ogling his wife.

Before Faye or Dizzy could say anything, Steven walked to the middle of the room, ringing a bell to get everyone's attention. "Let's gather back around so we can start the next session." He rang the bell again, then stuffed the long handle in his back pocket. Thankful for the interruption, Faye grabbed Dizzy by his hand and walked with him to join the rest of the group. "Just so you know, we'll meet here in the mornings before we break off into groups. Everyone should know their name, and make sure you go with your leader when they call you."

Dizzy looked at Faye then mouthed 'Heat,' the word printed on their welcome folder.

"What we're gonna do for our inaugural exercise is let the husbands talk first." His announcement was met with playful boos and hisses from some of the wives. "I know, I know—it's not what some of you want to hear, but I promise, if this is done right, those of you who aren't too happy now will be very pleased when this is over."

There were twenty-five couples at the retreat, ranging from a few years married to golden anniversary. Each husband had been instructed to stand up and introduce themself and their wife, then describe the day they met them and how it made them feel.

They heard about the Johnsons meeting in third grade and how Mark Johnson wasn't sure what he felt about Amber, but he felt a little better after he knocked her book out of her hand. Then he felt even better when she hit him in the face with a ball during an intense dodgeball game the next week. He'd been in love ever since.

The Harpers met at a bar twenty-five years ago, and according to Todd, he felt his hangover first, then said, "Oh shit," when he noticed Debra sleeping next to him.

Frank Duncan said he felt butterflies when he first met his wife, Susan. She came up to him after he was too scared to make the first move at a work convention ten years ago. He said he felt the ground shift. His story made a few of the other wives smile and coo at his honesty. Susan looked a bit frazzled but smiled through his story.

Forty-five minutes later, Steven stood up and clapped his hands together, rubbing them as he spoke. "Well, it looks like we have one more husband left. Once he's done, we'll break off into groups and meet here in the morning after breakfast." He sat down and motioned with his hand for Dizzy to stand and take his turn.

"Um... When I met Faye, it was the first day of our jobs. She was outside trying to muster up enough nerve to go into the building." Dizzy looked down at Faye, who was looking up at him. "It was cold that day. She was wearing a purple peacoat that matched her shoes and bag. I remember having to decide if I should wait for her to go in or walk around her and leave her out there looking all goofy. But then the wind picked up. She wasn't wearing a hat, and the diamonds in her ears were shining too bright for me to leave her out there with all the people on the street and her looking like a deer in headlights outside of the building. So, I waited. I introduced myself, and we talked for a bit. I liked her smile and the way she said her name. Faye. It kind of floated through the air. And her eyes were gorgeous. You could tell how excited she was. I was there for my first day the same way she was, but her excitement was kind of contagious. If I had to walk in with anyone else, I might not still be there, but getting to walk in with her and her pretty smile, shiny new bag, and a name light as air makes waking up for work worth it every day."

CHAPTER 8

Two miles into their five-mile hike, Dizzy was struggling. Faye was, too, but she decided one of them needed to be strong. When Steven ended the group meeting, leaders started calling group names. Faye and Dizzy followed the leader shouting Heat until they were outside with four other couples.

When they started, the scenery was ideal. Lush green grass, tall shady trees, and a well-walked dirt path right out of the movies. They were told by their leader, Jamie, that walking together was a part of marriage some people forget. This was an exercise in togetherness and endurance, like a long, successful marriage.

"How are you—" Dizzy stopped to catch his breath, panting as he put his hands behind his head. "Not about to pass out?"

"Trust me, I'm struggling," Faye said, holding her side. "But if I pass out, how am I getting back?" She put her hands on her head and continued walking. "We can't both be laid out." The terrain fooled them. What started out flat had morphed into more hills than they could count at mile two. "After sleeping in that bed, I'm not about to be sleeping on the ground 'cause I can't make it back."

Dizzy laughed, thinking about them on their backs, unable to get up. "I thought we were both in pretty good shape. All that bending you were doing this morning didn't prepare you for this?" he huffed out quickly.

"No, and neither did those weights you lift, Mr. Strongman." She took the water bottle he offered her and gulped down half before handing it back. "I don't do yoga in hiking boots and cargos." She tapped her watch, and the screen lit up. "We have three more miles to go." Dizzy looked at her and squinted. "What?"

"You really wouldn't carry me back if I passed out?" He leaned forward and put his hands on his knees, trying to regulate his breathing.

"How do you expect me to carry your big ass, Dizzy?" She laughed at his shocked expression.

"We're supposed to be working on our marriage, Faye. You can't leave your husband behind. It's a rule." He stood up straight and walked closer to her. Four inches taller than her, she was forced to look up to meet his eyes. "I think it's in the vows."

"Rule?" She took a step to the side before adding, "Fine. If you pass out, I'll roll your ass down the hill and meet you at the bottom."

He nodded with a laugh. "I'll take it."

Faye signed and moaned, closing her eyes at the immense pleasure she was feeling. "Oh my God, Dizzy. Your thumb is magic. Press harder."

They'd managed to crawl back to their room an hour ago,

finishing their five-mile hike by pure will and a few prayers. When they got back to the room, all they wanted to do was curl up on the most comfortable spot on the plush thick carpet and sleep for a few days, but Jamie, the group leader, advised they utilize the hot tub to soak their aching muscles. She left out the part where they'd have to lift their legs over the top to get in. So, with strength they weren't aware they had left, they pulled off their clothes and managed to get in the bubbling hot water wearing only their underwear.

Seeing Faye's dark wet skin against the dandelion color of her satin and lace bra and panties was a treat Dizzy didn't realize he deserved at the end of such a sweaty, literal uphill battle of a day. When her foot bobbed to the surface of the water, he distracted himself with it, taking it in his hand to massage, focusing his attention on her toes and the soles of her feet.

"Like this?" Dizzy asked, pressing the pad of his thumb into the arch of her foot. He was enjoying her reaction to his massage as much as he enjoyed having his hands on her.

"Yes!" Faye curled her toes, enjoying her massage. "I might be too relaxed to get out now." Her head was leaned back on the ledge, leaving the column of her neck the only thing visible to Dizzy. "I've got a confession," she said seriously.

Intrigued, Dizzy responded. "I'll bite, but remember, I'm holding your foot. If you tell me some silly shit, or you're a spy who hates fish, I'll pull you under." He raised his eyebrows, then gently yanked on her foot to show he wasn't kidding.

She lifted her head. "No, Dizzy, don't. I love Cecily and Miles. They're my betta besties." Laughing, she purposely omitted the spy part to test him, then yelled out, "I'm not a spy!" when she felt his hand tug on her calf. He let go of her leg, and she quickly tucked them underneath her butt. "Today was my first time hiking, ever." She released a breath as if her confession had really been weighing her down. "I always wondered why anyone would want to walk through the woods with birds and squirrel droppings, but I really enjoyed it." The shoulder shrug she gave him ached, so she sunk low into the water to soothe them. "The fresh air was nice, don't you think?"

"Fresh air is always good. You didn't take nature hikes as a Girl Scout?" He lifted his hand, inspecting his fingers for wrinkles.

"I was never in the Girl Scouts. What makes you think that?"

"You have the look. Plus, you're the most responsible person I know. Isn't that one of the Girl Scout rules? Pledge?"

Faye flicked water in his direction. "I don't know shit about rules or pledges. I was never one because my mom didn't like the uniforms or the cookies." Francine made it clear the first time Faye asked that no daughter of hers would be caught wearing a patch-covered sash when designers were readily available to create clothes. "How did you get all that from me liking the fresh air?" Faye looked at Dizzy's face as he stared back, looking her over. "You're used to it, though, aren't you, country boy?"

Giving her a smile, Dizzy reached for the leg she'd unconsciously untucked and pulled Faye to him with a yelp from her, followed by a couple of curse words and ending with her laughter. They were both too busy laughing to notice she'd landed in his lap. "You got a problem with your husband being a country boy?"

Faye blew out a breath at what was under her hands. Seeing his chest was nothing like having it against her own, so hard and strong. The flutters she felt in her belly surprised her. His grip on her hip was holding her in place, but his deep chocolate brown eyes seemed to cement her where she was. She wasn't prepared for the sparks to burn the way they did. This was Dizzy, her work partner of five years. So what if he knew more about her than any other man she knew, or she'd met his mama, sister, and niece? He was Dizzy. The way her body wanted to wrap around him at that moment didn't matter. Neither did the fast beat of her heart or the watering of her mouth as she looked at his lips, so succulent she would bet money they were pillow-soft when kissed or when sucking on her n— "No." She shook her head to clear it. "I don't have a problem with country boys."

"What about your husband?" Dizzy's hand slid from her hip to her knee as Faye pushed off of him, suddenly feeling too close and too hot with him and the bubbling water. She felt like she was going to burst into flames. Why did he have to ask her like that? Weren't they pretending? He was blurring the lines, and if she didn't get away now, those lines would be erased.

She stood up in front of him, meeting his eyes as he looked at her. "I'm gonna take a shower."

He tilted his head up to keep his eyes on her face since he was eye-level with the satin triangle of her panties he wanted to reach out and touch so badly. His eyes didn't move until she turned around and walked away, the thin yellow fabric clinging to her wet ass swaying from side to side. He exhaled, wanting to kick himself for asking her questions as if they were actually married. Up until now, it had been playful between them, jokes and good-natured flirting. Was this the right time to try for more? He wiped his hand down his face. This was going to be a long two weeks.

CHAPTER 9

The night was long for both of them. They went to bed, feeling more unsure than ever. The carefree morning of yesterday was gone. He and Faye were walking around each other like strangers, but he wouldn't take back what he said to her last night in the hot tub. Her water-slicked skin in his hands had opened a door for him he'd jammed closed the day they met, and now, the hinges were blown completely off. All he had to do was get Faye to walk through with him.

He wasn't sure how easy that was going to be.

"Ahh, there they are," Steven said. He waited for everyone to sit before speaking again. "This morning won't be as long as yesterday. We have one short exercise, and then, you'll break off into groups. Yesterday, you all hiked a few miles." There were groans from almost everyone in the room. Dizzy flexed his foot to stretch out his sore calf. "If this is your first time being here, you'll learn fast that each class or group exercise has a purpose. Some subtle, some not so much. The hike was a test in endurance. Most of you made it." He clapped two times. "Some of you decided going back was easier than heading for the finish line. Those of you who finished; congratulations. You made it together. You didn't quit. You relied on one another to make it 'til the end."

There were 'awws' and chuckles throughout the group—a few kisses among those who finished and folded arms and side-eyes from those who didn't.

"Right now, we're gonna have the wives stand up and say one word to describe what they wish for their marriage from this day forward."

Like the night before, the Johnsons went first. Amber's word was *fulfilled*. There were a myriad of words to that effect spoken from the rest of the wives: *satisfied, hopeful, content.* When it was Faye's turn, she took a deep breath, then smiled before looking at Dizzy and saying, "Exciting."

The group activity was going to start with another hike. Everyone groaned when Lisa, the leader for the day, broke the news.

"Don't worry," she reassured. "It'll be a short hike. I'll give you fifteen minutes to change into your bathing suits and meet me by the back door."

"Well, I guess those complimentary flip-flops we got will come in handy," Dizzy said, trying to get Faye to laugh. To his delight, she giggled, letting him know he hadn't crossed a line last night. "I'll go get my trunks on so you can have the room to yourself."

Dizzy rushed through changing his clothes, thinking about shopping with Faye and how much fun they'd had. Stepping into his swim trunks wasn't as exciting as before. Before, he had Faye waiting for him on the other side of the door to show. Now, he didn't know if she would be there or not. The lime green and polka dots didn't seem as fun without her. He found his shoes and grabbed a towel, then left the room. He didn't see her near the door, so he walked toward the group, hoping to see her there.

"How'd y'all do yesterday?" Russell asked. He was standing next to Justine, both of them in red. "I think we were one of the last couples to make it," he laughed.

"We did fine," Dizzy answered, stretching his calf again. "Way more walking than what I'm used to, but we made it." He smiled, thinking about the little pep talk Faye gave him.

"At least you came prepared with the hiking boots. I was wearing my J's. Shit's ruined now."

Dizzy laughed with him but didn't actually care. They all had a chance to change clothes before they left. Russell should have known better. He saw Lisa standing by the door, checking her watch. She looked up, moving her lips, doing a headcount of the people she could see.

"Hey, girl!" Justine shouted past Dizzy. "You ready for today?"

Dizzy looked behind him and saw Faye walking up. She wore a button-up shirt over her swimsuit, so all he could see was her long brown legs and the cherry red polish on her toes. "Hey," he said softly.

She looked at him while running a hand over the top of her hair, smiling. "Wish I knew we'd be doing this today. I would have done something with my hair."

"It looks great," Dizzy said, feeling hopeful since she was at least talking to him. He'd watched her hair grow from the small afro she'd met him with to what it was on most days, reaching high about her head like a crown fit for a queen. Even now, with her cornrows, he thought she looked majestic.

"Okay, guys," Lisa waved a hand in the air. "Let's make our way over here so I can see who we're missing."

Dizzy followed Faye's lead to the door where fifteen other

couples stood waiting for the next instructions. He stole glances at her face, trying to figure out what she might be thinking. Her eyebrows weren't raised, so she wasn't sorting through her thoughts. He didn't see her chewing on the inside of her cheek, so she wasn't weighing her pros and cons. She'd hum when she had to do something she didn't want to do, and he didn't hear anything but the murmur of the gathered people.

"We're gonna walk about a mile, then we'll be at our destination. I'm keeping it a secret, so no one backs out, but you'll see soon enough."

Following Lisa, they all walked east through the thick green grass. There were no trees today but an open field which seemed to go on forever.

"This is better than yesterday," Dizzy said, feeling left out without Faye talking. She'd been quiet since they joined the group. She didn't respond. He looked to the sky, the bright sun not quite high enough for it to be noon, then stopped walking. Faye walked about ten more steps before she stopped and turned around. She walked back to him, asking what was wrong with her eyes. "I can't take you being so quiet." He took a deep breath as the others got further away from them. "Talk to me, Faye," he said, looking into her eyes. He missed her. "I need to see my wife's smile again." He stood there, waiting for her to say something. Instead, she started pacing in front of him. "Faye."

She held her hand up to stop him from talking. "Hold on a minute." She paced back and forth, starting to create a path in the grass. "Last night, in the hot tub." She turned. "You were touching me—and I liked it." She stopped to gauge his reaction. He was stoic, allowing her to get her thoughts out. "And I know this is our job, and we're pretending, and it's fucked up for me to think this. I need you to tell me this is one hundred percent pretend, and I need to check my feelings." She continued pacing, looking at him every three steps she took.

"Is that what you want?" he asked, amused and relieved they were feeling the same. She didn't stop pacing. Dizzy stood up and stopped her with a hand on her arm. This was Faye. She talked her way through things when she wasn't sure what to do; she rambled when she was totally lost. "Faye." She looked up at him, her eyes pleading with him to tell her what she needed to hear to figure things out. He didn't know the words to tell her, so, on instinct, he prayed his actions spoke loud enough for her to understand. He kissed her. He pulled her into him by her arms, pressed his lips to hers, and held them there until he felt her relax. Her arms went slack, followed by a small moan, then her lips parted, allowing Dizzy to move his mouth to capture her bottom lip. When he felt her arms around his shoulders and a soft hand caress the back of his neck, he pulled her closer by her waist and deepened the kiss, adding his tongue and a small moan of his own. When they pulled away, they were both smiling and trying to catch their breath.

"So, I don't need to check my feelings?" She pressed her lips together, still tasting Dizzy on them.

"No, Mrs. Freeman. Those feelings of yours don't need to be checked." She closed her eyes and laughed, and he placed a kiss on her forehead. "Come on. We gotta catch up."

No one noticed when they joined up with the rest of the group. They were too busy looking at something Dizzy and Faye couldn't see yet. "What's going on?" Faye asked no one in particular.

"We're cliff diving," someone answered.

Dizzy watched Faye's eyes widen, stunned by the news. Heights had never been her thing; she hated them as much as she did spiders. She was the reason he had the desk by the window in their eighteenth-floor office. "What do you mean by cliff diving?" He placed his hand on Faye's shoulder to calm her down some. She'd started biting her lip, so he could tell she was worried. As if everyone heard him, the group started moving to create an opening for Dizzy and Faye to see. The field that seemed to go on forever actually stopped and was now a drop-off above clear blue water.

They stood back and watched each couple start to take off their shoes and undress to get ready to jump as if they hurled themselves off cliffs regularly.

"I'm not going to force you to jump. If you'd like, you can stand near this big rock and wait your turn," Lisa shouted. All eyes looked to the rock, contemplating. "We have lifeguards in the water just in case, but we've never had to use them." She looked around at all the scared, tepid faces and continued. "This is an exercise in trust. How much do you trust your spouse to make sure you're on the same page to make the right decision as a couple? As you fling yourself off this cliff, are you doing it with the person you trust the most? The person who you want to be with as you breach the water into the unknown?"

"She said we don't have to do this," Dizzy said to Faye as they walked away from the group. "We can hang back and cheer for all the others from this safe spot on the ground."

"No." Faye shook her head and started unbuttoning her shirt. "We're gonna do this. How many chances will we have to jump off a cliff?" She shrugged out of her shirt, revealing a white bikini top underneath, and cut-off shorts she started pulling down her legs.

Dizzy tried not to be jealous of the strings tied into bows on her hips, but the way the knots pressed into her skin and the loops hung down, brushing against her, he wished it was him. His eyes traveled up to her waist and the distinct line of fabric at the top, the smooth skin of her soft stomach, and the way her belly button sunk in. The further he went up, the faster his heart beat, until it almost stopped when he got to her top.

"Shit, Faye. I thought you said you had a bathing suit." Her breasts snugly filled out each thread of the triangles making up the top.

"What do you think this is, Dizzy?"

He looked around to see who was looking. Greg from Arizona was staring at her ass. "Say, man," he yelled out before switching their positions, so he was in Greg's direct line of sight.

"What's wrong?" Faye asked.

"This is not the one-piece I was expecting." He moved his hands as he spoke, waving them over the front of her body. "This...this is—" He wasn't sure what he wanted to say, so he stood there with his mouth open.

Faye took his silence as an objection. She had just decided to see what could happen with them, and Dizzy was a jealous ass. She was too old to be asking for permission to wear what she wanted. Her hand went to her hip, and she twisted her lips. "Dizzy Freeman. This is my bathing suit. I like two-pieces. If you have a problem, then we got a problem. Have you ever tried to go pee in a wet one-piece?"

His laughter caught her off guard. "This is sexy as hell, and I'm not mad at it." He looked over his shoulder to see Greg still looking. "Where'd you get shorts? I thought you were packing all pants."

"Had to use that knife for something. I cut up a few pairs." She adjusted the tie on her hip. "We good?"

Dizzy swept his eyes up from her toes up to her hair, licking the corner of his mouth. "Yeah, we're good."

They heard Lisa yell out, "Next!" and watched Greg and his

wife, Carla, walk up to jump. Only three other couples were waiting for their turn. One couple sitting off to the side had decided not to jump. Greg and Carla walked side by side to the edge then leaped together, knees tucked in front of them. The splash they made could barely be heard, but the cheers from the swimming couples who'd gone before them couldn't be missed.

They waited another twenty minutes as the other couples went. Then Lisa looked at them and motioned with her hand for them to step up and take their turn. Faye took three steps back, waiting for Dizzy to join her.

"You're sure about this?" he asked, standing next to her.

"Yep," she answered nervously.

"Okay, you two. They're ready when you are." Lisa stood off to the side, smiling at them.

"On three," Faye said, taking Dizzy's hand. She took a deep breath and started to count slowly. 1... 2... 3... They took one tentative step together, then five quicker steps toward the edge, hearts pounding loud against their chests. There were four more big steps before they could jump when Faye stopped, yelling, "Wait, wait, wait!"

Dizzy dug his heels into the ground to stop his progress, then looked back at Faye with concern. "Did you change your mind?" he asked, panting. "I said we don't have to do this."

"I want to. I just don't know if I can." Faye walked to the edge and looked down. "That's a lot of water, Dizzy." She walked back to him, shaking her head.

He stopped her before she could walk another trail in the grass with her pacing. "Faye, I know you, and I know you're trying to talk yourself into it, but I'm telling you, we don't have to do this." He rubbed her arms with his hands to soothe her. "We can go over there and sit with the other couple who didn't jump and be fine."

She shook her head. "No. We're gonna do this." She walked back to where they started. "I need you to give me a pep talk."

"A pep talk? I'm not gonna talk you into this if you don't want to." The look she gave him said he better get to talking. "Okay, okay." He looked around, trying to think of the perfect words to say. "Remember the nerve it took for you to tell me how much you wanted me?" He moved out of the way of her swatting hand. "I'm kidding," he laughed. "But you remember having to work up the nerve, right?"

Faye nodded. "Yeah, it took a few hours."

"This is the same as me and you. We're jumping feet-first off a damn cliff, Faye. I got you, and you got me. What do you say? Want to jump off this cliff?"

"With you, yes!"

"Then let's do the damn thing."

Faye stepped closer to him and tilted her head up to kiss him. "Okay." She stood beside him, taking his hand. "1... 2... 3!" They took off at a sprint toward the edge, the blue sky in their view, and the cool water as their target. With one final step, they both jumped off the edge, hand in hand, into an uncharted new world.

DIZZY

Union on Fire

marriage retreat

the sheets are so soft **14 days**

write about the retreat
write about the retreat
write about the retreat

Winner gets the cover

~~he was so hard~~
~~his body was so hard~~
his <u>muscles</u> were hard

he kissed me
soft pretty lips
beautiful body

We jumped off a fucking cliff!!

Mrs. Dizzy Freeman

CHAPTER 10

Faye hadn't laughed so hard in years. She'd replayed the jump in her head and her scream on the way down at least a dozen times. She'd never hear the end of it. She still couldn't believe she'd done it. They'd done it. Together. Took a running leap through the air past a point of no return, both off a cliff and in their relationship. The drop seemed to go on forever, but once their feet breached the water, it was absolutely worth it.

"Diiizzzy!!!"

They laughed all the way back to their room, partly in amusement, but mostly out of avoidance from when they came up from under the water. Faye had wrapped her arms around Dizzy's neck and her legs around his waist. His body responded immediately, but being the adults they were, they'd ignored the evident hardness between them, even as the small waves pushed their bodies closer together, pressing and rubbing Faye's center harder into Dizzy.

"You screamed the whole way down," Dizzy laughed. Faye turned her head to look at him, but he stopped her. "Keep still. I'm almost done."

She wished she could turn her head more and glare at him, but his hands in her hair felt too good. She was first to the shower when they got back to the room, taking her time to wash her hair, making sure any errant amoeba were washed away immediately. She'd praised Dizzy for slipping his shampoo and conditioner in his bag because the slip and hydration felt amazing. When she left the bathroom with a towel wrapped around her hair and a thick bathrobe on, Dizzy was sitting on the bed waiting for her. He smiled, stood up, gave her a quick kiss, then walked into the bathroom to take his turn.

When he offered to do her hair for her, she was skeptical, but he assured her he knew what he was doing. His fro was almost as nice as hers, so she took a chance.

"You really didn't bring anything for your hair?" Dizzy asked.

"I thought we were preparing for the end of the world." He raked his fingers through her hair to detangle, then picked up the next section. "Besides, I knew I could count on you to bring something if I needed it." She sighed, closing her eyes at how gentle his hands felt. "Where did you even learn how to do this? I mean, on someone else besides yourself."

They'd known each other for years, and he probably spent more time with her than anyone else, but there were things he'd never told her. Not secrets, but personal information he'd kept close to his heart. "Well, Ella hasn't always been the bubbly, smiling woman you know."

Growing up on a farm, his big sister had been the one to teach him how to ride a bike and a horse. She was the fearless one, the one who loved to compete and show off. Standing up on a horse was nothing to her. Hanging off one to run after a fleeing steer was even easier, but one errant plastic bag and a spooked horse had her flying through the air, landing with a broken left arm and a fractured shoulder on the right. Their parents were able to bring in a nurse who bathed and washed her hair, but that was the extent. Feeling bad for his big sis, he took over her haircare, teaching himself how to detangle, moisturize, twist, braid, and anything else she requested. By the time she came out of her slings and casts, he was an expert.

"You do Billie's hair too?"

After Ella's divorce, some days she couldn't bring herself to do her own hair, let alone Billie's, so Dizzy stepped in again, taking up the slack to help out his big sister. "If she asks me to, I will." He finished detangling the last section, then began to part Faye's hair to start twisting it. "You don't have any of those bobble things she likes."

"Bobbles?"

"Those colored balls with the elastic." He shrugged, not knowing what else to call them. "That's her name for them. She likes the big hot pink ones." He gently pushed her head to lean against his knee, then started to make the first flat twist.

"I never imagined I'd be sitting here, getting my hair done by Dizzy Freeman." She laughed, then drew in a breath to quiet down. "Who knew those fingers did more than peck away at a keyboard?"

"They're quite nimble when they have to be." They were quiet again for a few minutes before Dizzy spoke again. "Why do you think it took us so long to get here?"

Faye wasn't sure if she had an answer for it. Sure, they had agreed to pretend to be married, but they never agreed to kiss. That happened on its own. Like it was meant to happen. Maybe it'd been a long time coming. "Could be we needed an extra push."

Dizzy nodded. Looking across the office at Faye year after year had become the norm. Why fix what wasn't broken? Or was he too scared to get into something that would change their whole dynamic? "Calling you Mrs. Freeman was definitely a push. I guess I should thank Shannon for the mistake she made. For doing what I was too slow to do?"

Faye tried to turn her head again, but being in the middle of twisting her hair, Dizzy wouldn't let her. "Have you been trying to wife me up?"

"I'd have to start by asking you out first."

"Why didn't you?" She held her breath, waiting for his answer.

"If I had asked you two months ago, would you have even considered it?"

Faye had to admit she wouldn't have. They worked well as a partnership. Why change that? Why allow her mind to think it should be changed? "No," she answered honestly.

"I might seem like a tough guy, but having my heart broken by you would've really done me in."

"You think I'd break your heart?" Faye whispered.

"I think—" He quieted for a bit. "I think I'm done."

Faye ran her hands down the twists in her hair, not sure if she was happy he was done since she'd gotten comfortable with the warmth of his leg against her side or frustrated he didn't finish his thought. "Thank you," she said, getting up to walk to the mirror. "You did a great job. Billie's a lucky girl." She turned around when she saw his reflection walking toward her.

"You'd most definitely break my heart," Dizzy said. "Not because you wanted to or did it on accident, but because I would let you. I would have given you my whole heart without thinking about it. Then, when it was too late, you'd see me trying to tape that shit back together. And it'd be what I deserved because I let it happen."

"I'm not in the business of breaking hearts." She pulled the top of her robe closed as he stepped closer. "Not yours," she said against his lips. Dizzy was every good thing about all the dates she'd ever been on all rolled up into one. She wasn't rushing to get home at the end of the night or fantasizing about how fluffy her towels felt after taking them out of the dryer. She was with Dizzy, where she wanted to be.

"I appreciate that, Mrs. Freeman."

The kiss was gentle. Soft. A promise for their future and a vow to protect and safeguard each other's hearts.

"I should get to bed. We're cooking breakfast in the morning." She could have stood there in his arms all night, but her body wanted to lie down. Dropping through the air had caught up with her.

"Yeah, okay." Dizzy stepped back, understanding but disappointed. He watched her cross into the bedroom, then turn toward him.

"You want to help me build a pillow wall?"

CHAPTER 11

Dizzy hadn't slept in a bed with another person in months. The last time was purely by accident because he fell asleep before he could ask the woman if she wanted him to call an Uber for her. He liked his space and all the room he had to stretch out. His mom labeled him a wild sleeper at six months old, and he's been throwing his arm across the bed and kicking the covers off ever since. As he lay on the too-comfortable mattress, on his stomach with his arm hanging off, his fingers brushed the soft shag rug on the floor —a position he'd woken up in many times before, only this time he couldn't figure out why his leg seemed to be floating in the air.

A shift in the bed made him turn his head toward the movement, only to be met with a stack of pillows. He chuckled as last night rushed back to him. They spent thirty minutes deciding the best way to stack the pillows so they each had an equal amount of the bed and the pillows wouldn't fall over.

Looking down the bed, he saw his foot on top of the pillows. When he lifted his head above the wall, he saw Faye was asleep on her back, the satin purple and yellow scarf she wore down near her eyes. He took a few moments to watch her. Her lips formed a pout, and her arm was raised over her head, her fingers twitching. She made a small sigh then turned to her side away from him. Still wrapped in her robe, it pulled tight against her when she turned, giving him a close-up, unobstructed view of her pretty ass. Remembering who he was, he got up and went to the bathroom.

Faye was awake when he walked back into the room, brushing his teeth. "Morning," he said, trying to keep the toothpaste from spilling from his mouth.

"Hey." Faye closed one of her eyes then smiled before letting out a yawn. "Why's it so bright in here?"

"It's morning," he mumbled. He went to the sink to spit and rinse, then came back, wiping his mouth with the towel covering his shoulder. "You didn't close the curtains last night." He wanted to add she was too eager to jump into bed, but that seemed unnecessary and wasn't entirely true. "I guess cliff diving had you forgetting things."

"Are you always so happy in the morning?"

He laughed while walking to the end of the bed, standing at her feet. He watched her open her eyes, then close one to look at him. She tried to tuck her legs up out of the way, but he was too fast, already pulling her by the ankles.

"Dizzy!" She sat up, throwing her scarf at him. She laughed when he pulled it down over his hair.

"Hurry and get dressed. We have to get to the morning meeting. Hopefully, it won't take long cause I'm hungry." He bent down, placing his hands on her knees. "Cooking class, remember?" She nodded and groaned. "I thought food got you excited?"

She pushed him away so she could stand up. "I didn't sign up to cook."

"Just hurry up." He flicked the end of his towel at her calf, amazed she dodged out of the way so swiftly.

"Gotta be quicker than that, Dizzy Freeman."

"We're gonna keep it simple this time with an easy crêpe you can eat sweet or savory. Does everybody have an apron?" Bridgette, the cooking instructor, looked to the people of the class to see if anyone held their hand up for an apron. When she didn't see any, she continued with her welcome speech. "Earlier, at the morning meeting, you were asked what partnership looked like to you. In marriage, a partnership can make or break you. Are you a team player, or are you only playing to make yourself look good? Are you keeping score? My grandmother always used to tell me if you and your husband can cook together without breaking any dishes or one of y'all ending up with egg on your face, your marriage is solid." Dizzy chuckled behind Faye as he tied her apron behind her back, giving her hips a squeeze when he was done.

Bridgette went on to list the ingredients they should have to make sure everyone was starting with the same thing. Faye raised her hand even though they had everything.

"What kind of milk is this?"

"Regular whole milk. Do you need an alternative?" Bridgette asked.

"Yes," Faye answered. Dizzy was surprised she'd said anything. He would have kept his aversion to dairy milk to himself and powered through the food, but he was glad Faye said something. Bridgette handed them a carton of almond milk. "This is the good stuff," Faye said. When Dizzy looked at her, wondering how she knew, "Habitat for Humanity," she answered his silent question. "You told me the story of you giving up cow's milk."

They'd spent a week with hammers and nails in their hands building houses, early mornings and late nights to get three houses built on schedule. The second morning, they met at the breakfast tent, bowls in hand to get cereal. Dizzy ate his dry because they didn't have soy or almond milk. When Faye asked about it, he told her about the saddest day on the farm. One of the cows died delivering her calf. They couldn't get the calf to take any other milk, so it ended up dying too. The next morning after its death, Dizzy couldn't bring himself to drink any of the milk offered. He was too broken up over where the milk came from, and it kept him from drinking it again.

Dizzy looked at her, amazed. "You remembered that?"

"It was a sad story." Faye poured the milk into a measuring cup. "I almost hugged you after you told me, but you were funky." Her laugh cut into their somber moment.

"We were all funky, Faye. No one smells good while building a house." He started to crack the eggs and took the whisk she handed him. "Shouldn't you give me a kiss for being mean? Especially since you didn't give me one this morning." The corner of his mouth lifted in a sly smile as he watched her eyes dart around his face.

"I hadn't brushed my teeth yet."

"I know. It's why I kissed you on your forehead." He laughed at her scrunched-up face. The other couples were already pouring the batter into their pans, and they'd only started whisking. Even with his stomach starting to growl, he was having more fun than he'd ever had in a kitchen. With anyone.

"You're gonna be back on the couch tonight."

Knowing she was kidding, they got to work. She showed him how to tilt the bowl just right for whisking by standing beside him and miming with her hand. The wrinkles in her forehead showed he wasn't doing it to her satisfaction, so he put her in front of him and let her lead. Placing her hand on top of his, she pressed down to apply pressure and let up when he got to the turn. He probably did it for longer than he needed, but both of them liked their positions too much to stop. They heard a loud, hard "ahem" and looked up to see multiple sets of eyes on them. "Eyes on your own paper!" Dizzy shouted, turning away from them.

"It's time to pour. You want to start heating up the mushrooms?"

Reluctantly, he took a step back. He hated the separation immediately. Faye pulled out the chopping board, then handed him the colander to rinse the mushrooms.

After she chopped her fourth clove of garlic, he asked, "I thought you didn't cook?

"I don't. Doesn't mean I don't know how." He laughed because that was typical Faye behavior. She never showed all her cards at once. It was probably why he was still so eager to follow her around like a puppy. He couldn't wait to see what she'd reveal next. "My mom made sure I learned the ins and outs of a kitchen so I could take care of a husband." She rolled her eyes at the thought of it all. "I figured out, after the third date she set me up on, a husband should be able to take care of themselves. If I was asked if I liked to cook on a date, I was done."

Dizzy remembered the way his sister refused to learn anything having to do with the kitchen. If it involved more than opening a can, she wanted nothing to do with it. He, on the other hand, had his own set of measuring spoons when he was sixteen. Some of his fondest memories of Billie were of them in the kitchen together, telling bad jokes, laughing, and making messes that ended up in tasty food. He loved the process of mixing ingredients until they became nourishment for the body.

"Sorry, but your wife isn't a chef."

"You seem to be doing alright. Besides, you have a husband who won't let you starve." He picked up the ladle, scooping batter, then poured it into the pan, making sure it was spread evenly. He worked intently, making sure it was ready before he turned it.

Faye looked on, impressed with his skills. "Didn't I just help you whisk batter?"

Dizzy sucked in his bottom lip to control his smile. "That was fun." He plated the crêpe and smiled.

"You are definitely sleeping on the couch tonight."

Dizzy handed her a spoon so she could sample the filling before he put it in the crêpe. The way her mouth opened and wrapped around the spoon made him smile. She closed her eyes and hummed at the flavor as she swallowed. Before she could tell him how much she liked it, he was kissing her, using his lips to open her mouth to feel the texture of her tongue. She moaned, and he pulled her closer before quickly releasing her, resting his forehead on hers. "It needs more pepper."

CHAPTER 12

"*We got the golden ticket.*" Faye had been singing that phrase for an hour, leaving Dizzy to wonder if she knew any of the other lyrics. After the cooking class, Bridgette awarded three couples with golden tickets to be used later in the day. She didn't explain anything more but told them to come dressed to swim. She promised Faye no cliffs would be involved. There were lots of cheers and some 'of courses' from the other couples as the tickets were handed out. Bridgette also told them since they won, they didn't have to attend the group meeting that night.

"What do you think it is?" She didn't give him time to answer before she started ticking off what it could be. "A midnight swim? *We got the golden ticket.* No, something might get us in the water. Have you seen a sauna? Think we should take our towels? What if it's a private beach? *We got the golden ticket.*" This time, she waved the shiny rectangle in the air. "Horseback riding. Did you see horses? Nah, they told us to wear our swimsuits, so we're probably doing something else. Some secret exclusive bikini beach party. We still have a few hours of sunlight—" Her sentence was cut off by Dizzy's lips on hers, silencing her ramblings. "I guess it doesn't really matter." She suspected he'd learned the easiest way to shut her up when she was talking her way through uneasy excitement was to kiss her. She'd be mad, but his lips felt too good. They didn't meet hers with a hard pucker. He kept them soft and full, covering hers with his, then kissing her bottom lip, biting it gently before stepping away. The look of craving in his eyes made her weak every time.

"Why don't you go get dressed so we can find out?" Dizzy, already in his swim trunks, walked to the front room to give her some privacy and his body some time to cool down.

Faye rushed to put her swimsuit on, then stopped in front of the mirror to examine her face. She couldn't put her finger on it, but she looked different. Smoothing her hand over her hair, she smiled at the twists Dizzy put in. She swiped her fingers across her cheeks, still full. It wasn't that. Her eyes might have shined a bit more—maybe it was the bathroom lighting. She tilted her head to the side, then turned her body so she could see her ass in the mirror. Still fat. She smiled, then tried to press her lips together to stop. It just grew. She couldn't help it. She was incredibly happy. What started as a shocking mix-up was becoming a full-on jolt to her system she welcomed with open arms, especially if Dizzy was filling them.

Dizzy was waiting by the door when she walked out, looking suave and lean even in his lime green swim trunks. He'd put on a tee-shirt that stretched across his chest, and the quiet moment she had with herself in the bathroom suddenly felt like a bad idea because he looked good enough to lick, and she had to force herself to keep walking so they'd leave the room where it was safe.

A tall, thin man wearing green and blue swim trunks with a
matching headwrap spoke as they entered the dimly lit room.
"Good evening, welcome in. Please hand your tickets to Trina,
then stand by the wall to the left." Trina was a tall, curvy
woman wearing a white halter top bikini that struggled to hold
in her round ass cheeks. They followed the other ten couples to
the wall after handing off the ticket. Dizzy took Faye's hand and
placed her in front of him as the others crowded along the wall.
"My name is William, and I'll be your instructor tonight. While
you were all at your classes today, your instructors were
watching to see which couples worked the best together. If a
problem arose, how did you handle it? Did you smile more than
frown? Did you look at your cooking partner as if they hung the
moon?" He walked the length of the couples on the wall,
noticing their positions and posture—how close they stood to
each other if a loving hand was placed on a hip or shoulder, or
in Faye and Dizzy's case, fingers laced together at their side.
"You ticked off all the things your instructors were looking for,
so you're about to be awarded some quality alone time."

Faye looked up at Dizzy and shrugged. If they wanted alone
time, couldn't they have stayed in their room? He gave her
shoulder a squeeze, telling her to hear him out.

"As you can see, there are circular platforms on the floor,
each covered with fabric. They're actually floating beds and are
attached to the ceiling, so they'll rise off the floor with the push
of a button. Husbands will choose one and have a seat inside."
William grabbed a rug from the back of a nearby chair. It was
round and the same color green as his shorts. When it was on
the floor, he finished with his instructions. "Husbands, you're
gonna have a seat with your legs out in front of you. Make sure

you get into a comfortable position because you'll be sitting there for a while." He sat down, adjusting for a bit, then put his hand out for Trina. She sauntered close and took his hand. "Wives, your seat will be on your husband's lap." There were a few giggles when Trina stepped over William's legs with one foot, then slowly lowered herself onto him. "Make yourself comfortable." There were more giggles throughout the room as William used both his hands to pull Trina closer by grabbing two handfuls of her ass. "Ladies and gentlemen, you have won an exclusive semi-private makeout session."

William told them their ease together in the kitchen should flow into their prize. Although it sounded easy, he went on to explain this was an exercise in self-control and intimacy. Being in your husband's lap wasn't an invitation for exhibitionism, he warned. Although married couples usually had no problem when it came to sex, some of them forgot what it was like to court and just kiss. "So, enjoy yourselves. Mind your hands," he warned. "You're not the only ones in here. We all have ears, and the thin fabric doesn't make you invisible." He gave them all a huge grin. "Later, when you get back to your room, your night will be amazing."

"I can't believe you're grinning so much," Faye said, looking at Dizzy sitting in front of her. He was bouncing his knees like a kid watching his favorite candy bar being unwrapped. His hands itched, waiting to get the sweet taste on his fingers.

"Hurry up. We only have an hour and a half."

"Don't you think that's enough time for kissing?" He didn't answer, only stared up at her, waiting. She dropped her shorts, then pulled her shirt over her head, letting it fall to the floor.

"God damn. Faye."

"You like?" She turned to give him the full view of another bikini, this one light blue with small pink flowers. Then, with her feet on the outside of his knees, she took a few steps closer to him to get into position. Just like in the hot tub, his face was lined up with the junction at her thighs. Even above him, she could see how excited he was by the way his cheekbones jutted out. "Stop smiling so hard, Mr. Freeman."

His hands snaked up the outside of her thighs to usher her down. Once her knees touched the floor, she used her feet to move closer. They were belly to belly when Dizzy moved her legs to circle his waist and his arms to circle hers. "I'm glad you thought we would be learning how to survive the end of the world and decided to pack bikinis." She opened her mouth to respond, but he kept talking. "You always have made good decisions." His eyes darted down, then back up again. The light blue fabric seemed to brighten her cola-colored eyes, even in the dim room.

"I have to admit, I'm nervous." Dizzy's hands inched past her knees to her thighs again. "I feel like I'm sneaking away with my boyfriend while my parents are in the other room."

"You seem like the type." She swatted him on the arm, and he moved his hands up to her butt and pushed her closer to him. "I'm kidding. I'm sure you were a good girl." Faye felt the flutter of his lips against her collarbone. "You're with your husband tonight, so you can be bad if you want."

"Just kiss me, Dizzy."

He started low, leaving a trail of pecks along her collarbone. From one side to the other, her skin tingled with each press of his lips. He lingered at that little dip in the center, then inched his way up with his tongue. Wet and warm, he didn't stop until he was at the tiny spot behind her ear that made her moan. Her hands went to the back of his head to keep him there, then she released him, not wanting to be greedy, suddenly feeling an erotic shyness at how good he made her feel.

"You liked that?" Dizzy asked, trying to meet her darting eyes. "Tell me what you like, Faye. I'm good at following directions."

She knew that. She also knew Dizzy didn't need directions when it came to this. The way her body felt, he may as well have written the book. She was hot all over, and his lips hadn't even touched hers yet. "Yeah, that was good." He went back to the spot, making her moan again, this time sucking on it too. His thumbs made circles on her stomach while his hands palmed her hips, tightening his grip the faster he felt her heartbeat. "You're enjoying this, aren't you?"

"You have no idea, Mrs. Freeman." He lifted his head, waited for her to open her eyes. "You're not?"

She watched his eyes as they studied hers. He was waiting for an answer—an honest one, the only one he'd accept. She'd seen this expression before from him, one that questioned his sanity at the same time as portraying his absolute self. He was the most genuine when he had this look. This look was what he wore when the action of saying 'you have to believe me' was all in his face. "I think you know I am."

Maybe to prove a point or to turn the knob up another notch, Dizzy smiled and finally kissed her lips. He also pulled her closer to him, right against him. Her legs tightened around him, and the memories of the cliff dive came back to her. In the water, she'd felt how heavy he was but chose to ignore it. Now it was just the two of them, and it was too big to ignore. Faye could also tell he wasn't trying to hide it. He wanted her to feel it. He pulled her closer again, then used his hands to guide her hips up and down along his dick, as if he knew exactly where her clit was, and where to aim it was a bullseye with every tilt up and each tilt down.

Their kiss deepened as their moans got louder, then quieted

down when they remembered where they were. She let him lead, and soon, their lips weren't touching at all as Dizzy licked and sucked on her tongue, moving his hands up her torso. When he captured her lips again, he made her bottom one a priority, sucking and nibbling as she moved her hips on her own against him. She was wet and didn't care one bit if he felt, heard, or smelled her. His hands continued their climb, inching past her ribs until his fingers grazed the bottom of her bikini top.

"Wait." Faye's eyes widened, and she pulled her face back. She was right there. Dizzy was letting her ride her way to Euphoria City along his long, wide highway, and she needed to find a detour before the entire room knew exactly when she'd reached her destination.

"I'll stop."

"No. Yes. Shit, Dizzy. You've got my mind all jumbled up. Hands at a respectable place." His hands slid back down to her hips. "Just let me think for a second." His fingers felt too good. She wanted to feel the pads of his thumbs brush against her nipples, then pinch, pull, and twist when he added another finger. "Shit."

This wasn't just a kiss or a pep talk helping her face a fear of heights. This was getting her off. Letting her use his well-equipped body for her personal gain. There was absolutely no turning back from this. They couldn't chalk this up to an experiment once they were back in the office. This was the real deal.

"This will change everything, Dizzy." He kissed along her jaw, and she lifted her chin so he could go back to her neck or her spot he found so effortlessly before. He had his tongue on her pulse point, flicking the tip of it to the beat.

"Is that so bad?"

"What if we can't recreate this at home? What if it's this

place?" She was doing that thing where she talked herself out of things, except instead of pacing, she'd started moving her hips again, pressing her pulsing clit against his hard dick. "What if —"

"What if it was always meant to be?" he countered. "Maybe we needed William's class to push us in the right direction."

"What if I say I'm scared?"

"Of me?"

She was scared of this new feeling. This feeling her feet were giving her to stay planted where she was, where Dizzy was, to not run away because there was no reason to. She was safe, and she was happier than she'd ever been, and it would get so much better if she allowed it to. "Of us. Of taking this next step."

"I'll let you set the pace." Hearing her soft moans, he leaned back on his hands, willing to watch, resigning control to allow Faye to get herself off on her own. "I'll keep my hands at a respectable place and let you have it."

"Dizzy," she moaned softly, her orgasm pleading for release. "Yes, Mrs. Freeman?"

She lifted his hands to her breasts. "I won't tell if you don't."

His thumbs grazed her nipples as he softly sang, "*We got the golden ticket.*"

we got the golden ticket

a makeout session

??where they do that at??

→ here ←

↑

his tongue is magic

Dizzy's body is so hard

Mrs. Dizzy Freeman

write about the retreat

I can't believe I did that

retreat related!

retreat related

retreat related!

it felt so fucking good!

long wide highway

CHAPTER 13

At the morning meeting, Steven told the hikers to look for trinkets to represent them as a couple. Something from nature that was significant to both of them. So far, all Faye and Dizzy had gathered was a giant leaf Dizzy was trying to convince Faye was shaped like a mouse.

"Look at it like this." He held it up and tilted it to the side. "It looks like the one you used to have. Remember, you kept having to replace the batteries."

Faye didn't look convinced at all. She took the leaf from his hands and let it fall to the ground. "No, Dizzy." Placing her hands on her hips, she looked down at the dirt and other fallen leaves around them. "It has to mean something to both of us."

They continued walking. The slow pace Dizzy set for himself seemed to be working. This hiking trail wasn't kicking his ass as much as it did last time. Plus, Faye's faster pace was giving him an incredible view of her ass and thighs in the cargos she'd cut off.

"I'd think someone your age would be able to walk a little faster," Faye shouted from in front of him.

"Hush, old woman." Faye stopped, turned around, and

placed her hand on her hip. Dizzy knew he had about seven seconds before she turned the tables on him with a snide comeback. He jogged up to her before her mouth could form the words and kissed her into silence. "I'm kidding." To hammer it home, he kissed her again. "I like flat land, not all these hills. Too much damn climbing."

Faye smiled, thoroughly convinced. "You want to turn back? We don't have to do the whole trail this time."

Taking her hand, he took a few steps forward. "No, I'm good. Look what I found." He handed her a thick, knotted stick.

Looking at it, confused, she raised her eyebrows then waited for him to explain.

"What does it look like?"

After a few more minutes of staring at the stick, she started to laugh. "It looks like an ass."

"Booty camp, remember?"

Faye's mouth turned into a wide grin, then she laughed, loud enough to startle nearby birds. "It's perfect."

Although they were smiling and seemingly happy, they hadn't talked about what happened the night before. As they started to walk, he asked, "You doing alright?"

"I'm good."

"We should probably talk about last night." He captured her head between his hands before she could move her focus to the dirt beneath them. "Talk to me, Faye."

Her feet tapped the ground as if she wanted to walk away or pace back and forth, but the hold Dizzy had on her kept her where she was. "You slept on the couch," she said sadly.

When they got back to their room after their makeout session, Dizzy went straight to the bathroom, leaving Faye alone in the bedroom. He wasn't trying to be rude, but watching her ride out an orgasm was almost too much for him. He wasn't even sure how he walked back to their room upright. He hadn't meant to stay in the shower for so long. He'd decided on the way back to the room he'd take the coldest shower he could, then come out and talk to Faye. The freezing drops of water on his skin did nothing to eliminate the massive hard-on he had. What had worked before when he thought about Faye didn't have the same effect after she had been in his lap, the lingering warmth of her skin against his and the way her breath quickened the closer she got. The sounds she made stayed in his ears, drowning out the spray of the shower. He still felt the vibrations along her throat as she moaned while he kissed and licked at her skin, with its light taste of salt and smooth texture. He wrapped his hand around his dick, unable to stand the strain anymore. As he moved his hand up and down along his shaft, Faye's face was in his mind. The way her eyes squeezed shut tightly when she knew what was coming. The way her mouth opened slightly, then closed before opening again for her to bite her bottom lip. His hand continued, up and down, then a swirl of his thumb along the tip weakened his knees, making him hold himself up with a hand on the shower wall. He could hear her again, feel how hot her pussy was through the thin fabric they both wore. As much as he loved watching her come undone, he wanted to bury his face between her legs more. Taste the scent that surrounded them, let her nourish his body. He could feel it now. He pumped his hand faster, up and down, letting Faye's moans get him there. On the downstroke, with a squeeze of his hand, he finally came. Pearl-colored spurts of cum, one after another, washed away down the drain as he stifled his moan. It wasn't until he let go, letting his softness fall against his leg, that he finally felt the cold water.

"You were asleep when I got out of the shower."

"You still could have slept in the bed." She looked down at

the ground and kicked the dirt with the heel of her boot. "If things are gonna be weird between us, tell me now."

"Things are great between us, Faye. I've never been happier. Well..."

"Well, what?"

He had planned to go to the grave without telling her he was jacking off in the shower while she was on the other side of the door, but honesty seemed to be what she needed, so she wouldn't doubt what they'd started. "Look, I, uh... I had to take care of things in the shower."

"You're having second thoughts, aren't you?" She let go of his hand and started pacing in front of him.

Six steps, turn; six steps, turn. He watched her do it five times before blurting out, "I was rock hard and had to take care of it." He held her by her arms, trying to ignore the small smile forming on her face. "Seeing you in the bed only brought it back, and I wasn't about to take another shower or tap you on the shoulder to get rid of it." He took a step back, exhaled. "Trust me, Faye. I'm in this 100%."

Faye's smile was a full-on grin as Dizzy watched her open her mouth and press her lips together. Then she laughed. A roaring, deep-from-the-belly laugh had her wiping her eyes and bent at the waist, trying to catch her breath. She put her arm out when she saw Dizzy's feet walking past her. "Wait! I'm— I'm sorry." He stopped, but it took her a little longer to stop laughing. "I'm sorry." She took a cleansing breath to compose herself, then grabbed his hand. "I don't mean to laugh. It's just — You looked so scared to tell me even after I rode your shorts for almost an hour last night. I came on you, Dizzy. A tap on my shoulder would be what you deserve."

"Really?" The shocked expression on his face almost made Faye laugh again, but she swallowed it down quickly. "I mean, that's good to know, but I'd never do that."

With a small step forward, she leaned up and kissed him. "I know," she whispered. She pulled the knife from her side and smiled. "Watch this."

Dizzy looked on as Faye started to carve into a nearby tree. When she was finished, he chuckled to himself. Her whispered reply just a few moments ago had brought back memories of the sounds of her soft, drawn-out moans. Moans he knew he'd never forget, that right now were making him hard again. "Let's head back before I change my mind and start tapping."

CHAPTER 14

"**I**'m sure you're all tired from your hike, so this shouldn't take long. Hopefully, the air and cardio have cleared your mind enough to answer the question. Is there anyone who'd like to go first?" Steven stood in the center of the room, looking at them for a volunteer. Dizzy sat next to Faye, playing with the inside of her wrist, trying to make her laugh. Someone on the other side of the room raised their hand, but neither of them noticed, especially when Dizzy made Faye giggle when he whispered in her ear. Dizzy saw Russell stand up and start talking but didn't hear anything he said. Faye held all of his attention. Four more people stood up before Faye's name was called.

"Umm, I thought you were calling on the husbands?" Faye asked.

"Decided to switch things up a bit," Steven said. "Besides," he smiled, "it looks as if your husband is a little occupied at the moment."

Dizzy placed a kiss on the inside of Faye's wrist. "Oh," he said, noticing his audience. "My bad." He let her hand go and followed her with his eyes as she stood.

Faye linked her hands together nervously. Talking in front of a crowd wasn't her strong suit. The reason she liked writing was it gave her a voice without saying anything out loud. "Well, I guess..." She looked at Dizzy shyly. "I chose Dizzy because he makes things easier."

"In what way?" Steven asked.

Faye thought back to the day they met. Her nervous excitement kept her standing in front of the building in the cold, but then Dizzy showed up, and she was able to walk through the door. He'd been by her side more times than she could count. Each time, she would think about how great a friend he was. How lucky she was to have a friend who would put her comfort and happiness before his own. If she was having a bad day, Dizzy made sure she didn't wallow in it too long. He'd been the one constant in her life who made sure to ask, *'You alright?'* every day.

"There was a time about three years ago when I wasn't sure about a lot of things, especially myself. No one seemed to notice except for Dizzy. I understand people have lives and worries of their own, and I was okay with working through my shit on my own, but then Dizzy was there, telling me I didn't have to." Faye met Dizzy's eyes and wiped at the tears forming in her eyes. "When my favorite actor died, he showed up with a few pints of ice cream and steaming hot French fries." Someone laughed near them, and Faye laughed too, remembering how she'd sent a text to her sister telling her about how sad she was he'd died and not getting any sympathy. She'd just decided on the movie she would start with for her remembrance marathon when Dizzy knocked on her door. He stayed and watched four movies with her while she cried on his shoulder through each one, stuffing her face with French fries and spoonfuls of chocolate chip ice cream.

"Aww, that was sweet of him," Regina cooed.

"Sorry to go off-topic, but Dizzy, what made you go to her?" Steven asked.

"When I heard about it, I knew she would be upset. I can't tell you how many afternoons she spent talking about him and his movies. He was her favorite. I've never heard anyone talk more excitedly about anything. She would have never called me and cried about it, so I did it for her."

"Aww!" Regina said again.

"I didn't mean to interrupt. Continue, Faye."

Dizzy could tell the moment she let it sink in that all eyes were on her. She pressed her lips together and took a deep breath, letting her shyness take over.

"That's all."

Back in their room, they were both quiet. Faye's revelation on why she chose Dizzy was on both their minds—not heavy, but lingering. He didn't want to pry more into what she'd told the group because she'd shut down. He knew she needed to ease into it on her own. Up until now, they'd only grazed the surface.

He sat down on the couch and watched her walk to the bedroom. When he heard the shower start, he sighed and stretched his arms on the back of the couch. Even though he wished she'd said something, he still smiled because he knew she would. He started to laugh when her singing floated through the air.

...this is what it sounds like, when doves cryyyy-ing cause I love youuuu-give good love to me, it's never too much baby you give good love- if it isn't love, why do I feel this way, why does she stay on my mind

He was writing in his notebook when she came out, wrapped in her robe. She smiled, then sat beside him. "I don't know about you, but I'm exhausted. That hike wore me out."

"You hungry?"

"Yes."

"I ordered some food for us to eat while we watch the movie." He gave her a kiss on the forehead then got up. "It should be here before I get out of the shower. Don't eat all the fries."

Faye's smile when he walked back into the living room made Dizzy wonder what good she was up to. "What's that look for? What'd you do?" He took a slow step forward, then paused to wait for her explanation.

She closed the notebook she was writing in. "You get things taken care of in there?" She looked at him for four seconds with a straight face, then burst into laughter, doubling over on the couch.

Sighing, Dizzy sat down, trying to ignore her. He dipped a few fries in the ketchup sitting in the small metal cups. Exhaling through his nose, he concentrated on chewing and the spiciness of the fries. It was a few minutes later when he realized he couldn't ignore her anymore, especially with her gasping for air between breaks of laughing. "Are you done?" He shook his head. "I never should have told you."

"That you were jacking off in the shower?" She bit her lip until her laughing stopped, leaving her with a goofy grin Dizzy loved. "I'm sorry I keep laughing about it, but it's seriously the most flattering thing anyone has ever told me."

"Really?"

"Yes! And the fact you let me do what I did without asking me to return the favor is the best part. I'm five times hornier now, imagining you—" she pointed toward the front of his shorts, "taking care of things."

"Shit. Faye. You're making this hard— I mean, not easy. I'm trying to be a gentleman here, not jump you like we're seventeen in the backseat of a car." He dropped the fries in his hand on the tray and looked at her. "I know we were pushed into this, but I'm trying to do this right."

The part of him that desperately wanted Faye's body underneath him right then was getting louder, nagging him about doing things the right way, especially since Faye seemed to be on the side of his nagging part. He needed it to quiet down so he could think clearly and stay on the path he'd set. Getting to pretend to be married was one thing, but benefiting from it with his dick was entirely different. He had convinced himself two weeks at a resort with Faye was like one long date, and when they got back, he could do things properly: pick her up for dinner, bring her home, give her a kiss at the door. But then she changed all that, turning their makeout session into an erotic dry hump he'd never forget.

"I'm telling you, you don't have to." Wiping her hands on her napkin, then taking a gulp of her drink, she said, "I confessed to a whole group of strangers why you mean so much to me. I'm glad we're here, Dizzy. Even if you're being an unnecessary gentleman."

"Let me try, okay?" His eyes were pleading as his hands flexed in an attempt to not reach out and touch her, feel her skin under her robe. "Okay, Mrs. Freeman?"

"Okay," she agreed. "Can I have a kiss, though?"

"Get over here."

After finishing with their burgers and fries, Faye felt better. Her burger was loaded with jalapeños and onions. She could taste the garlic they seasoned it with. It was amazing, but it also left her breath not fit for another makeout session, so she was cool with being his little spoon as they laid on the couch to watch the video Winnie said they'd need to familiarize themselves with before her next class.

"What channel is it supposed to be on?" Faye asked, scanning through the channels past infomercials, home shopping, and telenovelas. "I think she said something about a menu." Bringing the remote up to her eyes, she looked for a menu button, but Dizzy's long finger was there, pressing the 0 to take them to SB Network. "You think you're so smart," she said over her shoulder.

"Just find the channel. We'll probably fall asleep halfway through it, anyway." Dizzy yawned behind her, full from dinner and the exertion of the hike. He squeezed her tummy from behind, then let out a contented sigh while he waited for her to find the video.

"Here it is." They both looked at the narrow blue rectangle on the screen with the words *Release Some Tension* in the center. "Maybe this will show me how to get rid of the pain in my foot."

"It still hurts?" He slid his foot down her arch and watched her wiggle her toes.

"Yes, but I'll be fine tomorrow. No hiking, so I don't have to wear those heavy-ass boots." She pushed play, and they both went silent as they focused on watching the pixelated screen turn into the color green before swiping up and revealing a woman lying on a massive bed, her body covered with a thin sheet. Soft music played in the background, then the camera panned to an open window, with sheer curtains billowing from the breeze outside. The sound of the music rose, then another person appeared. "Why is he naked?"

"Why's he so shiny?" Dizzy asked, watching the oily, muscled man walk further into the room.

A soothing narrator voice started once the man was at the end of the massage table near the woman's feet.

This massage technique will teach you how to pleasure the yoni.

Faye gasped, slapping her hand over her mouth to stifle the laugh begging to come out from the feel of Dizzy going stiff behind her, and not in a good way. The thin sheet draped on the woman was slowly pulled down by the man, revealing her nude body. Faye was impressed by her flawless copper skin and delectable thickness. The man picked up a small glass container and started to drizzle it in his hand.

You'll want to start with an oil such as avocado, coconut, vegetable, or olive. These oils are great for massages and are also safe for the vagina and for eating.

Dizzy exhaled sharply, then moved half an inch away from Faye. She laughed, then closed the distance between them, making sure to wiggle her ass against him when she did.

Pour a generous amount of oil onto your hand, then starting with her feet, work your way up to the knees. Apply light pressure, listening for cues from your partner as to when more pressure can be applied.

Dizzy closed his eyes, hoping the darkness would help calm down his body. It didn't. Faye was the first thing he saw when they were shut. He could still feel the weight of her in his lap from the makeout session, her quiet moans against his neck. He tried to put more space between them, feeling his dick grow from the memories.

"You alright back there, Mr. Freeman?"

"Hmm..." Dizzy groaned, then rolled to his back. The slight bounce of the couch cushions from Faye's chuckles didn't help. "You're enjoying this, aren't you?"

"Very much so."

Chancing it, Dizzy took a deep breath and opened one eye to glance at the TV.

Caress her mound, let your fingers glide smoothly between her lips and folds. Concentrate on the sensation on your fingertips. This area is sensitive, be gentle, take your time. Remember to listen to her breathing, moans, and sighs. When she gives you permission, insert one finger inside of her.

"Okay," Dizzy huffed out. With the agility of a gazelle, he leaped over the back of the couch, adjusting his hard dick in the process. "I gotta take a shower."

CHAPTER 15

The restless sleep Dizzy got on the couch messed up his back. He could have happily sunk into the plush mattress in the bedroom, but with Faye sharing it with him, there was no way he would be able to keep his one-sided promise to be a gentleman and do things right. He still wasn't sure why he was trying to be so good, especially with Faye giving him the go-ahead to be as bad as he wanted. He knew he didn't want to use their assignment as a hall pass to get Faye into bed. This was never how he'd imagined it would go. In his mind, there'd be dates and long talks, small gifts just because, and laughs through movies at his apartment before they got to the sex. The regular steps you take while in a relationship, but before any of that could happen, they were playing happily married couple Mr. and Mrs. Freeman. In the past few days, they'd held hands, jumped off a cliff, and he'd willingly let Faye ride the front of his shorts to paradise. He wasn't sure how much longer he could hold out. Even with him saying it multiple times a day, the fact Faye was trying to coax him out of his clothes was making it difficult for him to stay the course.

"You know your neck wouldn't hurt so much if you'd slept in the bed last night. I would've kept my hands to myself."

Dizzy looked at Faye, who'd taken his hand as they walked to class. She was wearing a white tank top with the resort logo across the front with matching white spandex shorts. The resort had supplied them with clothes for the exercise class they were assigned to. Dizzy felt like he was getting dressed for sixth grade PE when he slipped on the tee-shirt and basketball shorts, both white like Faye's. "I don't believe you," he smiled, shaking his head.

"You're probably right." Faye pulled him toward a pair of wingback chairs off to the side of the common room. "Come have a seat, so we can talk real quick."

Reluctantly, he sat, nodding to the people passing by, then looked at Faye, giving her his undivided attention.

"I had a lot of time to think last night since I was horny and couldn't sleep." Dizzy thought her smile was too big and didn't match his self-induced agony. "As much fun as I had with you and that video, I'm gonna let up." She put her hands up in surrender.

Dizzy watched her mouth close, then waited for the punchline or for her to say something to contradict what she'd said, but it never came. "Just like that?"

"Yeah. I mean, I can tell I'm stressing you out, and—"

"It's not you, Faye." He stretched his arm out for her to take his hand. "You've never stressed me out. It's..." Dizzy raised his shoulders and looked around the big open space, then dropped them slowly, pulling her onto his lap. "Everything." Faye wrapped her arms around his neck, tickling his skin with her fingertips. Dizzy closed his eyes to focus, letting his nostrils flare, both loving and hating his decision to sit her on his lap. As much as he wanted to take her back to the room and give in, he was also incredibly nervous. Performance anxiety was creeping in more and more with each sly smile Faye threw his way. Never in his life had he been nervous or questioned his ability until now. "The more I think about it, the more I'm not sure." His hand swiped across his forehead. "You're designer shoes and five-star restaurants. I love my old cowboy boots and a two-day-old stew. What if—"

"You two are the cutest!" Regina's voice cut in. "Are you sure you've only been married five years? Ugh! You're made for each other, you know?" She didn't wait for them to respond before walking toward the doors to go outside.

They both laughed, not sure what to say to the sudden interruption before Faye asked in a sigh, "What if we ate stew together, wearing only designer shoes and cowboy boots?"

"Damn it, Faye." He shook his head and blew out a breath. Now he had a new image in his mind to add to his mental folder full of her.

"I already told you, I'm in," Faye said. "I also said I'm down whenever you are." She leaned in and kissed him sweetly. "Can we go exercise now?"

"Thank you for joining us today. Are you ready to sweat?"

Dizzy looked at the mirrored walls of the room and the reflection of the fifteen other couples in the class. The instructors, Sam and Sarah, were in the middle of the room, looking excited to see everyone. There was a large square towel underneath their bare feet on the foam-covered floor. Sarah's toenails were painted green like the rest of her spandex onesie. The word DRIP was printed along her thigh.

"As Sam mentioned, we will be sweating today, but our class is more about making our bodies feel good, making our partner's body feel good. We all know how beneficial exercise is to the body. It helps improve our mood and mental health. Mood is one of those things that affects our sex drive. We're gonna combine those things today."

Seeing the confused faces, Sam simplified Sarah's speech. "We're gonna do some couples exercises to get the blood pumping so you can get pumping in the bedroom." Sam chuckled, then looked over at Sarah, who was shaking her head.

Dizzy raked his hand over his eyes, hoping the entire class didn't hear his groan. The thread he was hanging by got a little weaker. He felt Faye squeeze his hand, offering some sort of condolence.

"We're gonna start with a warm-up." Sam sat down first, opening his legs into a V, then Sarah followed, touching her feet to his. They linked hands, then Sam took Sarah's wrists and pulled her arms toward him. They held the position for a minute before switching.

The rest of the class followed suit, stretching with grunts and sighs, a few curse words thrown here and there as thigh muscles were stretched. Next, they moved to the arms. Faye knelt behind Dizzy and lifted his arms to start the second stretch. He was well aware of how soft her hands felt gliding up and down his arms and the increased beating of his heart as he pleaded with his mind to tell his manhood to act like it had some sense and not show itself in this room full of people.

"Now, we're going back to the legs. Those of you who just stretched your arms, go ahead and lie back. Your partner should stay right where they are—spread your knees apart enough for your partner's head to fit in between."

The audible drawn-out "shit" Dizzy let out could be heard from across the room. Faye did her best, but she laughed anyway.

"Grab the back of their legs on your way down, so you don't hurt yourself. Their legs will be your brace as you raise your legs one at a time." They all watched as Sam demonstrated by holding onto Sarah and lifting his left leg. Sarah took his foot in her hand and pulled back slightly. "Don't pull too hard. We want to stretch, not pull it out of place." Sam chuckled, along with a few others. When Dizzy was in position, he closed his eyes, knowing good and well what he'd be looking at if they were open. He lifted his right leg for Faye to grab, hoping his hands by his sides, gripping the towel underneath them, would keep him from wobbling too much. They didn't. Instead of grabbing and holding onto his foot, Faye had to stretch her arm out to catch it, which threw her off balance, making her fall forward with an "Oof." When Dizzy felt her hands hit the ground next to his knees, he opened his eyes and was met with the sight of her crotch in his face. It took everything in him to keep from sticking his tongue out and licking the long seam of her shorts that ran from front to back.

A voice from above him kept him from doing anything inappropriate. "This is why you need to grab your partner's legs." Sarah was next to them, with her hand on Faye's back, keeping her in place above Dizzy. "Don't be afraid to hold onto them. Her thighs are stronger than you think." Sarah helped Faye sit back up, then placed Dizzy's hands where they should be. "Now try it."

He lifted his leg as he gripped the back of Faye's legs, trying not to think about the way his fingers sank into her soft skin or that her knees were at his ears. He heard Sarah ask if that was better, so he nodded, not trusting his voice to speak. Eight leg lifts on the right, then switch to the left. Faye's turn went a lot easier. She held onto Dizzy from the start, making it go by quickly.

"Now that we're all stretched and warmed up, we're going to start with some ab work." Sam was standing, then went down to both knees. "If you were on your knees before, stay. If you were on your back, go ahead and get in the same position as your partner, except in front of them." Sarah got on her knees with her back to Sam, then waited for everyone to mirror their positions.

Dizzy focused on the back of Faye's head in front of him, thinking whatever they were about to do, the twists in her hair seemed safe enough not to give him an aneurysm.

"Now, those in front," Sarah said as she started moving back. "Scoot back, so your feet are under your partner. You'll stop once your butt is touching their front."

Someone giggled to Dizzy's left. He turned to see who, but then Faye was touching the front of his shorts, and he couldn't concentrate on anything but how warm she felt.

"Partners in the back, grab those hips." The hair at the back of Faye's head moved from the breath Dizzy blew out. As light as he could, he placed his hands on Faye's hips, then waited for the next instructions. "Okay, now those in front, place your hands at the back of your head, elbows out." They watched Sarah do it, then followed. "What you'll do now is slowly lean forward. You want to get your nose as close to the floor as you can without falling. It's why you have a partner behind you. They're there to make sure you stay in form and don't hit the ground. It'll be face-first if your grip on those hips isn't tight enough." Sam made a show of opening and then closing his hands around Sarah's hips. "Watch us, then you try it." Sarah took a breath through her nose, then brought her chest down. You could tell she was relying on Sam to make sure she didn't fall. Once her nose was an inch from the floor, she exhaled then came back up. "You have to work as a team to get this right. If you're in front, your abs are what you want to use. Behind you, your partner is also using their abs along with their legs to make sure you stay in form and off the floor." Sarah did another one, then they waited until others joined them before doing a third.

"You ready?" Faye asked Dizzy.

"Yeah," he answered, not fully confident in his answer. Dizzy met her eyes when she looked back at him. "I'm ready." He felt the small jostle of her butt against him as she got set. As she leaned forward, he had no other choice but to grip her hard, pressing his fingertips into her fleshy hips. He watched her head move away from him as she bent forward, held the position for three seconds, then moved back up.

"You okay?"

He looked around at everyone in the zone, heads bobbing up and down as partners held tight, making sure they didn't fall. "I'm good."

Before she started her second descent, she wiggled her hips to make her knees more comfortable. In the process, she also wiggled his dick too, which had been being good so far, but as she bent forward, her ass decided good wasn't what it wanted. Dizzy was in the perfect position to feel both halves of her ass as she moved up and down, gliding against him with every rep. This was nothing like their makeout session. This was better. His hands were positioned just right to pull down those tight shorts she wore and push into her.

"Jesus," he whispered in a tortured voice. He couldn't take it anymore. "Faye."

"Yeah?"

"Let's go eat some stew."

CHAPTER 16

Getting back to the room took an agonizing amount of time. The steps to the bed took even longer. Faye had never wanted anyone on top of or inside her as much as she wanted Dizzy. The past few days had been the best kind of foreplay, and now, she was ready for the real show. She inhaled sharply when Dizzy's lips touched the side of her neck as he took a handful of her breast, pinching her nipple in the process. This Dizzy wasn't the one from a few days ago who said he wanted to take his time. The way his hands and tongue felt, Faye could tell this Dizzy was on a mission. What she thought was a one-sided, lust-fueled craving for her longtime co-worker was actually a mutual longing Dizzy was able to handle better than she could.

Those hands she'd watched for so many years, typing away at his keyboard, were now working in tandem to remove her tank top and pull down her shorts at the same time. This Dizzy was tired of waiting as much as she was. She liked this Dizzy. This Dizzy had her bent over the edge of the bed with a smack to her ass. He didn't say much, letting his actions do all the speaking. One hand grabbed the back of her neck while the other squeezed an ass cheek, spreading her open while pushing her head toward the mattress.

"Don't move."

The sternness of his command sent shivers through her. He'd backed away, the warmth of his hands noticeably missing with every second she waited. When she went to turn her head in search of him, his hand was at her neck, keeping her from moving, the other hand swiping a finger through the slickness of her pussy up to the crack of her ass. She wanted to moan at the feeling, but then Dizzy decided enough was enough and pushed the head of his dick inside her, trapping all those sounds in her throat. When he couldn't go anymore, he pulled out slowly, with a hiss, then pushed back into her. Faye could feel every inch from tip to balls and all the thickness in between. She finally found her voice and moaned low and long as he sank into her again and again. Dizzy staked his claim on her pussy, hitting a spot so sweet she never wanted his strokes to stop. They were steady, fast, and just what she needed.

"Right there," she whispered. "Yes."

She met him halfway, throwing it back to feel him a little better. He smacked her ass again—encouraging or cautioning, she didn't care. She was right there, and stopping wasn't possible. She squeezed her pussy around him, so he knew she was close.

"Don't stop."

He didn't. He started to move faster, gripping her hips and moaning when their bodies slapped together in their frenzy. Faye clutched the duvet with both hands. She could feel her thighs begin to shake.

"I got you, Faye," Dizzy panted.

That reassurance had her squeezing harder, moaning louder —thanking God she had a soft place to land underneath her because Dizzy was working her pussy like it owed him money, the only way to pay him was in orgasms, and he was charging interest.

The tingling started in her toes, then moved up to her belly until it reached her ears, then made the return trip, tickling her ribs before exploding. "Ohh..." she moaned before calling Dizzy's name. His name crawled slowly from her mouth a second time, then a third as she watched the white bedspread bunched in her hands, focusing on something to keep her from soaring too high, grasping for something to hold on to. Dizzy wrapped an arm around her waist, allowing her to feel each spasm of her pussy as he moved back and forth inside her, stroking her through her orgasm.

She hoped the deep breath she took once it subsided prepared her for whatever Dizzy had next. The delicious fullness she felt, the trickles of sweat that dripped down her back and chest, the sounds they'd created had her yearning for more. She wasn't ready for them to stop. The weakness in her knees and the steady pulse she felt in her pussy sent a signal to her brain she could take more. Dizzy's hand on the middle of her back, pressing down, made sure she could. With his next stroke, he'd reached a place foreign even to Faye, an undiscovered place no one else had tried to explore before. Swiping the tip of his dick across it, he unearthed its bounty, pulling more erotic moans from Faye as she started to come again. With one final stroke, he came too, staking his flag within her.

We consummated
our "marriage"

Mrs. Dizzy Freeman

he couldn't take
it anymore   I had it in his face
his mouth was right <u>there</u>

"Don't move"   stew ←
            stew ←
            stew ←

Dizzy was so hard!
            long and thick

he made me wait
it was worth   My "husband" had
every <u>horny</u>   me every way he
minute   wanted.

"pick your favorite position. We'll start with that
one when we get home."

CHAPTER 17

"**W**hy are you still laughing?"

Faye covered her mouth to keep the bits of lettuce and tomato from her taco in her mouth. "I can't help it."

Dizzy took another swig of the beer in his hand while trying not to look at her. They'd been in and out of giggling fits ever since they put their clothes back on. Dizzy was sitting on the bed in his basketball shorts, while Faye wore a robe. He would look at her, and Faye would laugh, causing him to laugh with her. He'd been doing good concentrating on the feel and taste of the seasonal beer they'd ordered an hour ago, but Faye didn't seem to care. Dizzy gulped down the last of his beer, then started to peel the sticky paper off the glass bottle. "You can stop at any time."

Sensing his irritation in the way he chewed on his bottom lip, Faye crawled over to sit next to him on the bed. She mirrored his position, stretching and crossing her legs out in front of her. She adjusted her robe to cover her knee, then moved to take Dizzy's hand in hers. He tried to move it away, but she wouldn't allow it. "Don't be like that," Faye said, looking at him. "Did you ever think we'd be here? Like this?" He was silent before slowly shaking his head from side to side. "Look at me, Dizzy Freeman. Have you ever seen me look like this?"

He glanced at her face, all dewy skin and hair flat on one side. It made the fresh memories of her head down and ass up even more vivid in his mind. His free hand moved to hide his hardening manhood so he could concentrate on what she was saying. "No," he groaned quietly, looking straight ahead.

"I don't think I've ever felt like this either. I—" Faye quieted to gather her thoughts.

Taking her silence to mean reconsideration, Dizzy asked, "Was this a mistake?" He knew it didn't feel like one. Not now after they'd consummated their fake marriage. He knew lust and desire clouded judgments, but he also knew he desired to be with Faye whether they were naked in the bed or fully clothed, reading a book. What she wanted was unknown to him, and right now, her silence seemed like they'd done the wrong thing.

"I feel like I should always feel this way. Elated and nervous and excited and anxious. You should've been taking my clothes off a long time ago." Climbing into his lap, Faye smiled at the wondrous look on Dizzy's face. "I mean, I don't know if I would've let you, but for the sake of arguing, you should have had me naked on one of our desks before today."

That brought a smile to his face. "The glass wall on our office says otherwise." Dizzy met Faye's lips when she leaned in to kiss him, pressing softly against her, letting his mouth linger for a bit before opening to taste her tongue and how it mixed with the remnants of the beer he'd just finished. It was the small movement of her hips that made Dizzy break their kiss. He used his hands to keep her steady. "So, you're saying?"

"You don't have to take so many cold showers now."

"Wow," Dizzy said, looking around, nodding his head. "It wasn't that many." He chuckled when Faye raised her shoulders to shrug. "You know I work with facts. Tell me exactly how you're feeling right now."

"I'm feeling this is exactly where we're meant to be. You and me kissing, touching, and exploring where this goes beyond this place."

"You said you were nervous and anxious."

"Yeah, but only because you've been right here all this time. I never thought of us as a possibility until we were in the hot tub in our underwear."

Dizzy's hand found a place to rest on the top of her thigh under her robe, and he smiled. "I've known—for a while." He caressed her skin with his thumb, debating how high he wanted to move it. He wouldn't dare say "for years," but it was the truth. She was the one who he looked forward to seeing when he woke up in the morning, even if he had to wait until he got to their office. Her smile made his day. Even her rants, when she was stressed, had become something to look forward to because he knew how to calm her down. Partnership seemed to be what they were best at. He just didn't know how to transition into more without losing their friendship because, in the end, she meant more to him than she knew.

"So, I guess we've got some catching up to do?" Faye asked.

Dizzy shook his head no, then scooted down flat on the bed, making Faye lie on top of him. "No," he said against the crook of her neck. "Starting here is perfect."

CHAPTER 18

The elevator ride up to the eighteenth floor was a quiet one for Faye and Dizzy. They'd been back home for a week, but this was the first time they'd been to the office, working within the confines of either Dizzy's apartment or Faye's house to finish their article and then separately when nothing was getting done but each other. Dizzy had every intention of brushing his lips against Faye's sweet spot as the elevator made its climb upward, but the sounds of steps and chatter from people entering after them had them separating and glancing at one another from opposite corners. As the doors opened to all the designated floors, they made their way back to each other and were able to steal a kiss right before the ding alerted them they'd reached their destination.

"This was ridiculous, Cheryl. Do you know what we went through?"

Kenny was ranting when they walked into the conference room. He looked like he'd just crawled out of the woods instead of been back at home for five days. Unlike him and Faye, who'd come in bright-eyed and bushy-tailed, Tiffany and Kenny looked haggard, worn down even. Dizzy hid his smile, imagining what the two went through for two weeks.

"Morning, everyone," Dizzy said, pulling Faye's chair out for her.

"What's all the fuss about?" Faye asked, already knowing the answer.

"Welcome back, you two," Cheryl said, looking at Dizzy and Faye. She focused her attention back on Kenny. "What exactly is the problem, Kenny?"

His nostrils flared as he stared at Faye and Dizzy. "You two enjoy your luxury resort?"

Instead of answering, they smiled at each other. Dizzy resisted the urge to roll his chair closer to Faye.

"This is funny to you?" Tiffany asked, scratching her wrist. "We spent fourteen days out in the damn wilderness all because of them." Tiffany pointed to Dizzy and Faye. "They took our trip while we had to suffer through hell!"

Cheryl looked between the two couples, confused. "Can someone please tell me what's going on here? Did something happen at the resort?"

"There was no resort!" Kenny screeched. "We ended up at the fucking Survivalist Boot Camp. Day after day of swatting away bugs, hiking through mud, sleeping on the ground, and eating squirrel stew." Kenny looked at Faye and Dizzy with fire in his eyes. "Do you know how tiring it is to eat stew every damn day?"

Faye was the first to crack. A deep bellow of laughter rang out, spilling into the hallway. She tried to stop, but Dizzy joined her, and she got louder. They were both out of breath and wiping tears from their eyes when Cheryl raised her voice.

"What is so funny?" She brought her hand down flat on the table to quiet them down. "Somebody better start talking."

For the next thirty minutes, Kenny and Tiffany went through

the hellacious time they had at the boot camp. How because they were sent to the wrong place, they had to suffer through roughing it, completely unprepared.

"We tried to call, but you and Shannon conveniently went on vacation when we needed you." Tiffany threw an accusatory glare at Cheryl. "I ruined my favorite Chanel flats, not to mention the two pairs of Jordans Kenny had to throw away. And can I ask how is it we were sent to the *wrong*," Tiffany put her hands up for finger quotes, "place when our names were on the registration list for the boot camp?"

"So, you two ended up at the Survivalist Boot Camp?" Cheryl asked Tiffany, jotting something down in her notebook. "And you two," she turned to the now-quiet Dizzy and Faye, "ended up at the marriage retreat?"

They all nodded.

"Shannon!" Cheryl yelled.

"Get her ass in here. This is all because of her. She did this on purpose," Tiffany whined. "We went through hell! Sleeping in tents! We packed for a relaxing resort. Not to learn how to hotwire cars, siphon gas, and make weapons from tree branches."

A smiling Shannon waltzed into the room, carrying her tablet, ready to take notes or orders, whichever was more urgent. "What can I do for you?"

Kenny started in before Cheryl could answer. "Don't come in here like you don't know how you fucked us over." He stood up and walked to the back of the room. "You had one job!" Kenny slapped his hands together, then brought his hand up to his forehead. "Get the right people to the right places. You messed it up."

"Calm down, Kenny," Dizzy said. "It's over. There's nothing she can do about it now."

Shannon stood, meeting eyes with everyone in the room. "I'm not sure what you want me to say?"

"How did they end up at the wrong place, Shannon?"

Dizzy watched Shannon close her eyes and cross her arms across her chest, holding her tablet against her. When she opened them again, she was glaring at Tiffany.

"For years, you two have treated me like your personal maid. Not once have you asked me how I'm doing or if I'm okay. All I get is, 'Shannon, this water isn't cold enough. Schedule my interview. Make sure I get the best table.'" Shannon placed her tablet on the table. "I don't know if you know this, but I work for Ms. Hines, not you."

"Bullshit!" Kenny shouted. "You work for whoever gives you an order."

"You're walking a thin line, Kenny," Cheryl warned. "Did something happen? I know it's been a week, but seems like you all got back okay." Her stoic expression only pissed Kenny off more.

"Barely," Tiffany whispered.

"I understand the situation wasn't ideal," Faye said, "but we all had a job to do."

Dizzy nodded in agreement. "The assignment was to spend two weeks at the boot camp or the resort and write about it." He understood where the Stuarts were coming from, but then again, they had a job to do. It was over, so there was nothing else to do. Them crying about it wouldn't turn back time and magically have them at the marriage retreat. "We did our part. Did you?"

"What the fuck you mean, did we? No, we didn't."

"You didn't write your article?" Cheryl asked, standing up. "We go to print in a few days. Why?"

The excuse Kenny and Tiffany gave wasn't good enough for

Cheryl. She didn't care that they'd had their heart set on a
relaxing resort, or Tiffany had shopped for a whole week to find
the perfect teddy to wear for Kenny, and it had to be used as a
patch on their tent to keep the mosquitoes out. Stories of
twisted ankles, wading through waist-deep freezing water, and
never having a moment alone took up the next forty-five
minutes.

Dizzy and Faye sat and listened, moving their head from left
to right between Cheryl reprimanding the Stuarts and them
trying to justify why they couldn't complete the job they were
given. With each rebuttal, Dizzy's chair inched closer to Faye's.
His hand was making its way up her thigh when his name was
called.

"Dizzy," Tiffany called. "Why don't you tell us what you and
Cheryl talked about before we left?" The confused look on his
face made her refresh his memory. "*I wish I could go with you*,"
Tiffany imitated Cheryl's voice. "Y'all got something going on?
Is this how they got sent on our retreat?"

"That is ridiculous," Cheryl answered. "And also, none of
your business." She gathered up her things to leave.
"Congratulations, you two," she said to Dizzy and Faye. "You've
earned yourself the feature story and cover."

"Where are you going?" Kenny asked, getting up from his
chair. She didn't answer, and when she turned to leave, Kenny
and Tiffany were right behind her.

Dizzy and Faye laughed, not feeling a bit sorry for the
Stuarts. They got up to leave when Shannon handed them the
box she had carried in with her.

"The retreat sent this over for you." Shannon looked at both
of them as they moved closer to each other. "Looks like you two
had a good time," she smiled with a wink. "I thought you
deserved a nice vacation."

"Thank you," Faye said sincerely.

Dizzy watched Faye untie the ribbon on the box, both smiling when she pulled out a small black basket containing a large bottle of massage oil, their golden ticket, and a black-framed picture of the heart she'd carved into a tree on their hike with the letters F+D in the center.

EPILOGUE

"Faye," Dizzy whispered, drawing out the name while kissing the shell of her ear. He moved his head back when Faye's hand swatted him away. He knew she wasn't fully asleep because he'd been up for an hour moving around, making noises to wake her up. "Faye," he tried again. This time, he licked her earlobe, working his way down to her spot, nuzzling into it, making her squeal. He knew she couldn't be mad after that even if she wanted ten more minutes of sleep. "It's time to get up." Slapping her ass, Dizzy moved to get up but was stopped by Faye's hand on his leg.

"Wait, don't stop," she moaned.

Dizzy laughed but stood up anyway. "It's getting late. Billie will be here any minute."

That got her up. Faye hopped out of bed, snatching her scarf off her head, then walked into the bathroom. "Why'd you let me sleep so late?"

Dizzy watched the jiggle of her ass cheeks as she walked away, then followed after her. She was brushing her teeth, glaring at him through the mirror when he stood behind her. "I thought you set the alarm," she mumbled around her toothbrush. "You're gonna have Billie mad at me." She spit, and her mouth turned down into a frown.

"You're one of her favorite people, so that's not gonna happen." He rubbed his hands over her hips and kissed her neck. "She's not coming to see us anyway. Probably won't even say hi when she runs in."

Faye's shoulders slumped, knowing he was right. "She's only coming for the babies, huh?" She watched Dizzy nod his head in the mirror. Faye took a deep breath, then turned around to face him. "Well," she tilted her head to kiss him. "For what it's worth, I think you're way cuter than them."

Twenty minutes later, Dizzy was opening the door to the blur of Billie rushing past him.

"Hey, Uncle Dizzy."

Ella was five steps behind her, gingerly walking in, sipping on coffee while her sunglasses covered her eyes. "It would take three of these," she held up her Styrofoam cup, "and a 40% off sale at Nordstrom to get me to move that fast."

"Morning, Billie," Faye greeted through a smile.

Ella gave her a kiss on the cheek before putting her purse down. "Faye, you know you are too pretty for my brother. I don't know why you settled."

"That's never been funny, Ella," Dizzy said.

For two years, his sister had been giving him a hard time about Faye dating down by being with him. Faye always laughed it off, knowing most of it stemmed from Dizzy moving away from Billie to research and collect stories for his book on Black farmers.

A tap on Faye's arm made her look down. "Yes, ma'am, Miss Billie?" Faye said to her bright smile. Being called Miss Billie always made her smile. She had been given the name the day after Dizzy and Faye came back from the retreat. She had so

many questions about why they were always together and why
Dizzy kissed her or touched her on her butt. To ease into the
right way to answer her questions, Faye started off with, "Well,
Miss Billie..."

"Can I feed the babies now?" Billie asked, looking up with
hopeful brown eyes. Faye stayed quiet longer than Billie thought
necessary, then nodded her head and took her hand. Faye
handed her the can of fish food, then watched her shake it in
front of the tank to call all the fish to the side.

"Not too much, Billie," Dizzy said, coming up behind Faye.
He wrapped his arms around her waist and rocked her gently
from side to side. Billie looked up at Dizzy, then turned back to
the tank. He snuck a kiss to Faye's neck.

"When are you headed back out, Dizzy?" Ella asked. He'd
come into town for the carnival, but she knew he'd be leaving
soon to interview more farmers.

"Long enough to convince Faye to go with me." Faye stepped
out of his arms to look at him. He'd asked her before, but this
time, the seriousness of his face felt different. This wasn't him
asking her to ride shotgun; this was him asking her to ride with
him forever. "What do you say? Feel like putting a few more
miles on my truck with me?"

Faye looked at Billie's eyes, and Ella's smile, and all the
bettas, who seemed to be staring at her too. She couldn't think
of a reason not to. She quickly tried to calculate how many
minutes were in forever.

"With you? Yes."

ACKNOWLEDGEMENTS

This story came about when I wanted to take a handful of tropes and make a sweet, fun story out of them. I tried to make this funny and frustrating, but rewarding in the end. I hope you enjoyed Faye and Dizzy and their journey to love.

Hendrix and Georgia, who thought they were being sneaky by writing booty camp on my outline board when I wasn't looking. Jokes on you, mom used it in her book.

My husband, who's never asked why I get heart eyes over fictional characters, or betta fish. They're never bigger than the ones I have for you.

My squad, who comes through every time I have a lump of clay of an idea, to help me sculpt it into my version of a masterpiece. I couldn't do any of this without you. Still can't believe how far we've come since that first week of fangirling each other.

Kia, who knows the minutes in the day better than I do. You're amazing and encouraging and an absolute treasure. I can hear your laugh all the way in Texas.

Thank you all for reading and sticking with me. They'll be more to come, but I write slowly, so I can't tell you exactly when.